IT

William Mayne

IT

HAMISH HAMILTON
London

First published in Great Britain 1977 by
Hamish Hamilton Children's Books Ltd.,
Garden House, 57–59 Long Acre, London WC2E 9JZ
Second impression February 1980

ISBN 0 241 89695 9

Set, printed and bound in Great Britain by
Fakenham Press Limited, Fakenham, Norfolk

For
Lucy

1

THERE WAS A STRANGE SKY for a strange day. Alice Dyson
could see it from the car, where she had been sent after
being in Sarrow vicarage for about three minutes when she
and Mum went there to bring Grandpa down into the city
for lunch.

Grandpa was vicar of St Michael's church on top of
Sarrow Hill, but he had to come down to the Minster six
times a year and preach, and this was one of the days, and
not quite an ordinary one either. He was less patient than
usual on this day. Alice had begun to do what she had done
several times before, that is, fold up his robes and put them
in a suitcase to bring down with him. But she had gone into
a dream and put a gravelly footprint on the sleeve of the
white surplice.

It proved how careless she was and that she had not
wiped her feet on the doormat either. Mum had sent her
out; Grandpa had dropped her down in his opinion again.
And this year, this time of it, in fact this very month, there
was not a great distance for his opinion to fall, so she was
down at nothing again.

Even the dream she had been giving herself had not been
good. Now she considered it was the nasty dream of a
nasty person. She had been looking round the room at all
Grandpa's things and realizing how hopeless it was to

expect to achieve anything for herself because he had already done it all, and there on his walls and shelves were the signs of it: the relics of foreign lands, the row of books he had written, and the signed picture of him holding hands with the queen; the things of a complete person who had completed everything.

Alice sat down again in the car, but in the back now, abandoning the faint warmth she had put into the front seat on the way up. She pushed her hands up inside the sleeves of the other arm's cardigan and looked out of the window.

The strange sky was like grey velvet, soft-looking cloud not far away, solid but streaked with light and dark so that it looked a little untidy and in want of steaming and ironing on the wrong side to become smooth. There was a hole somewhere, however, because a patch of sunshine was wandering over the town. From here she could see right across the roofs of it, a surface all of angles and textures and shades of red tile to blue slate and all at much the same height, like several packs of cards confused but smoothed out in a shallow mound on the floor. But standing out like sudden jokers were several tall black backs of Methodist and Baptist chapels, the Congregational church spire, and the two praying towers of St Cuthbert's Roman Catholic church, the single square one of All Saints, and, greatest of all, like the box the cards came in, the three towers of the Minster, which was a cathedral and where Grandpa was to preach that afternoon.

The patch of sunshine went among these buildings, along North Road and into the Market Place, being careful, it seemed, not to touch anything but the ground. It parked for a time in the Market, like other traffic, and then moved once more, straight up Kirk Alley, glittered on the Minster, picking it out in warm fire, and went again to the east and south.

Alice saw two things then. One was startling, and did not matter. The other was ordinary and mattered a great deal to her for some months, right from this day in October to some time the next May, across the winter.

The commonplace pretty thing came first. The sunlight sliding off the Minster showed some green fields beyond. And there, in outline against the glowing green was a small distinct hill crowned with small distinct bare trees, all sharp enough to be the only thing Alice saw for the several seconds the sight was in existence. The seconds were less than a handful, and then the sunlight had gone again and there was nothing she could pick out because all the distances mingled, more as if her eyes had failed than the scene had altered. It was nothing: the little hill had showed itself, and Alice thought it odd because she had not seen it before although it must be very near where she lived and she ought to know about it.

She forgot it, because the startling thing had happened to the Minster. It seemed to have fallen into ruin, as if the sunlight just now upon it had truly been a flame that had destroyed it. It now had no roof, and the windows gaped empty, the sky beyond showing through them. There was no mistake about it: Alice had seen numbers of ruined abbeys eaten out by time, and this was the very appearance.

"Yes, it has gone," she said to herself, out loud. She pulled her hands from her sleeves and clapped her left palm with her right-hand fingers. She was applauding the ruin of the Minster because it was an exciting thing to see suddenly, and doing it before she told herself she knew what had happened and that it hadn't happened.

Then Grandpa was between them and tugging at the car door, which she had tidily locked after herself when she got out. He was not pleased that it would not open while she sat inside and talked to herself and waved her arms about. Then of course the lock button would not come up while he had his thumb on the catch outside, so that she looked as if she were being silly about opening it. He rattled impatiently, and between rattles she lifted the catch, and he got in.

"You might have done better not to come," he said.

"I'll walk home," said Alice, knowing quite well she would indeed have done better not to come. She undid the lock of her own door and opened that.

"Thank you," said Mum, who was waiting outside with the suitcase. "Sit down," and she put the case on Alice's knees. It was hard, heavy, and painful.

"Now you've cut me," said Alice, watching the blood spout from her knee. But her vision was better than the facts, and there was only a small white dent where the hinges of the case had pressed.

"Be," said Mum, through her teeth, and loud, in a short and fierce form of saying Be Quiet. Alice worked out, while she was rapidly being quiet and not beginning to bleed, that talking to her like that might have worked when she was eight, or even ten, but not now she was nearly twelve; but of course it had. At the same time she finished realizing what had happened to the Minster.

Nothing had happened at all. The sky beyond it was the same colour as the lead roof, so that from this distance one merged into the other; and the windows, by some trick of light, and because they were half made of lead too, had looked like openings to the same sky. Still, she thought, it did fall into ruin, and just for me. Then she changed sides with the suitcase because that was easier than moving it about on to its base.

"You've turned the wrong way," said Grandpa.

"No," said Mum.

But Mum went on: "Matthew," she said, meaning that

she was driving this way to collect another person coming to lunch, Alice's brother. The remarks had not been about Alice at all, which was a good thing in some ways and annoying neglect in others. Alice sat alongside the case and felt she was alone. She remembered that feeling as the year went by and the next year went on into summer: today was her last day of being alone for all of that time.

"Beadlam," said Grandpa, looking from his side window. Most people would have thought he had made a mistake in some other word, but Grandpa did not make mistakes. "Beadlam Cross," he said out in full. Alice knew already what he was looking at and naming. The cross was a tall pillar of stone, either very rough or with worn old carving on it. It no longer had any arms. She had seen it before many times, most of them with Grandpa, who always commented upon it; and in her primary school days the class had walked up here and looked at it and been told something about it. She had not listened because the information had come from one of Grandpa's books, carried by the teacher.

"Beadlam," said Grandpa. "Bedlam, Bethlehem, hospital of St Mary of Bethlehem, perhaps; a madhouse in the old days." If he knew something he would nearly always inform you.

"I expect they told us at school," said Alice, meaning to be polite, interested and kind; but what she said sounded cheeky, insolent and pert. But she had heard him say it before and it was probably impossible to say exactly the right thing.

"You'd better not say any more," said Mum.

I'm in ruins too, Alice thought. The whole sky is the same colour as my mind.

No one said anything for a time. The car was going along country lanes just outside the town, on its way to Matthew's school. There was silence. There was an even stronger silence when they passed the lodge gate of St Hilda's School for Girls. At sight of it Alice resolved to have no thoughts at all for a few minutes. She allowed her throat to form the words "I was right," and felt them move against her collar, and that was all. To see whether she was right, and because there was no person she could talk to about it, she looked at the needles and gauges and measuring devices in front of the driver. She wondered why they did not register nought out of ten and instantly run out of petrol, oil, water, ignition, brakes and indicator. Dials on the backs of Mum's or Grandpa's head would have shown Empty, or Frozen, or Choke; though Grandpa's side was more likely to say Glove Box, because that was what his side of the car had.

They were a quarter way round the town now, and had turned in towards it. Alice looked out for the Minster, to see about the roof, but she could only see it from one end and no roof showed, as if the building were keeping up the suspense of the truth.

"Easter," said Grandpa.

"No, Mum, you're going east enough," said Alice.

"Cross," said Grandpa, completing his words, and looking out of the window at this second cross by the road.

"The hospital for cracked eggs this time," said Alice. "Not cracked people." But she said it quietly to the nails of her two thumbs. Then she changed her subject internally and looked out again at the Minster, which had moved up behind the houses and shown more of its side. Its roof had parted from the sky now and was in place once more; the ruin had recovered. Alice was glad, but mostly because the ruining had stayed private; no one else knew about it.

The car turned in at the yard of the Minster School, where Matthew was, and stopped.

"I'll go," said Grandpa and Alice together. But there was no need for them to go together, which neither of them would want, and no need to decide who had the best claim, because Matthew had been waiting inside the door and came at once, pulling on his cap and having to take it off again instantly and twice, to Grandpa first and then to Mum. Alice had nothing. Matthew got in, tipping the case over on to Alice's side, and beamed, which was something more than a smile and less than a grin.

"Getting put in today, then, Matthew?" said Grandpa. That meant Matthew was being asked about the afternoon's ceremony in the Minster, when he was to become officially part of the Minster choir, after his two years on trial. The little ceremony took place during the afternoon service, and Matthew was allowed out today for lunch because of it. Alice knew about the ceremony because she had seen it several times. She felt she really knew more about it than Matthew did, because, when she was small she had seen it happen to big boys, and when she was a little larger she had seen it happen to the boys her own size, and now she saw it happen to small boys, like Matthew.

Grandpa was now telling Matthew about the trouble he had had in arranging to preach one of his sermons on this particular day so that he could be there. Matthew was sitting and nodding his head. His expression was so firmly fixed on his face that it seemed polished on, making him unable to speak. So he had to nod. If Alice had nodded instead of speaking up there would have been trouble, unless she had not said the wrong things; but Grandpa understood and forgave Matthew, and was now exchanging beams with him. Alice thought they were exactly alike just now except that Grandpa was a thousand years old and Matthew a hundred.

Then she saw again the little hill she had seen outlined

against the sunlit fields. The car was passing it, quite near home, and close against the end of the Minster, and she was aware of it for the first time but still knew it had always been there beyond the wall, rising up steep as she had seen it, and covered with leafless trees.

"What's that?" she asked, pointing.

"The Eyell," said Grandpa, hearing her, looking out, but still attending to Matthew.

"I.L.?" said Alice. "I yell?"

"Eyell," said Grandpa, pushing down her interrupting arm, thinking no more of her but going on with his talk to Matthew.

Alice turned in her seat and watched the Eyell disappear, first behind the brick wall along the roadside right up against its foot, and then behind the darker brick houses of Eye Street, themselves crowded against the road. The roofs crept up the Eyell until the mound itself had gone, and then the brush of twigs on top held up a few marks on the cloud, and they in turn were wiped away by a passing chimney. The Eyell, and the Minster beyond it, had vanished.

"Alice, sit still," said Mum, because Alice was turning and watching, and rubbing the back window and tipping the case about, in spite of being able to see nothing more. She sat straight again. She thought she had finished with the Eyell, and that it was only a plain little hill after all. Perhaps she had finished with it, but it had not yet begun with her. It was to do so later in the day.

The car turned into Racecourse Road, and at the next corner was the house, at one end of the woodyard, and they were home.

2

GETTING HOME CHANGED nothing for Alice. She was still going to be the wrong way out for everybody else. She could see it in everything around her, and she could see it in what she did herself and in what she had ever done.

"I don't know what you are thinking about these days," said Mum, when Alice had stood and watched something interesting but fatal happen to the gravy in the baking dish. "You've burnt both." Alice had, of course. She had stopped stirring and let the gas flame scorch a ring, first of innocent bubbles and then of real cinder, while she had thought about nothing she could remember in words.

"You'll clean that drip-tin," said Dad, and there was another little argument about that, with Dad using one name for the thing, Mum the other and Alice not being allowed to be on either side.

"Out of my kitchen, both of you," said Mum, when it was quite clear that no one agreed.

"Now then," said Dad to Alice as they went out of the door, "have a care."

"I have several," said Alice.

"Happen you have," said Dad. Then they went to bring their visitors to the table. Grandpa was a visitor in a natural sense; someone who came occasionally. Matthew was a visitor too, and quite like a stranger. Today he was even an important visitor, and a popular one: everyone made a fuss of him, because everyone was pleased that he was going into the Minster choir. Alice was pleased too, but she could tell that her reasons were different. She was pleased because she loved him, which meant that if he was doing what he wanted to do then she was glad and proud.

But perhaps it might be better not to love him. Alice looked at him now, where he was sitting on the arm of Dad's chair rubbing his face and saying it hurt from smiling, and she knew she wanted him to stay at home now for a long time so that she could play Monopoly all the evening and have a fight with him as well. She thought about the rules for a fight and then left them, because there wasn't going to be one. Matthew was going to have lunch, go up to the Minster for a practice with the rest of the choir, go to Evensong with its ceremony, and then go back to the school in the school minibus, somehow cleaned out of her life except for occasional appearances.

"Ready to serve," said Mum, coming through from the kitchen.

"Dishing up," said Dad to Grandpa.

"I heard the text in the original Greek," said Grandpa, getting up. He put one hand behind Matthew and the other on Alice's back, to usher them to the table. Alice instantly turned into a tortoise with a hard shell and arms and legs drawn in so that it could not move. She knew at once she was being unfriendly and that Grandpa had come round to forgiving her. She changed her ungrateful attitude by going round Grandpa and helping to propel Matthew forward, which she did by twisting his arm up behind his back.

"Simmer down," said Mum.

"Side up," said Dad.

"Sit down and shut up," said Matthew, and everybody was pleased with that.

The meal began. The gravy was scorched, after being rescued by Mum. The others seemed to think it was the flavour it should be, but Alice scraped hers away and left it and took no notice of a slight shaking of Mum's head about the way she was doing it.

"You're acting disagreeably," said Mum.

"I'm not acting," said Alice. "I'm realling."

"I doubt you are," said Mum, and Dad said "I doubt you aren't," but they both meant exactly the same thing, only Dad used his town language and Mum used vicarage language that she had been brought up with.

Alice stopped doing anything with the gravy and poured herself a glass of water, slow and careful, right to the top and beyond the top but without spilling, with the water raised in a blister. The spilling came when she lifted the glass to drink from it, and a plunge of water ran down her chin and her thumb and the glass and splashed on her plate.

So for her the meal ended in the next minute, when she got up to take the plate to the kitchen and pour away the water, without thinking of the gravy, and Mum told her to come back at once, and Dad said Right Now, and Alice thought she would go her own way, and put the plate down on the carpet and went out of the room and sat on her bed, while her stomach made a grinding noise and sank empty away.

Much later Matthew came carefully along the passage with some apple pie for her.

"I don't know what it is," he said. "Mum said pudding, Dad says afters, and Grandpa says dessert and at school we say sweet."

"Apple pie," said Alice. "Go and get yours, Matt."

"We've had ours," said Matthew. "Are you going to come this afternoon?"

"I've seen them do it before," said Alice.

"Would you come to our school if they took girls?" said Matthew. "Then you could be in the choir too."

"They wouldn't have me," said Alice.

"No," said Matthew, thoughtfully and not in the least unkindly, "you didn't even get into that other school, did you?"

"No brains," said Alice. "I wish you'd brought a spoon, Matthew, because my hair's getting in the plate."

"You've nearly finished," said Matthew. "I think you didn't want to go to that school. You should have gone to St Hilda's, because it's our sister school."

"I'm your sister anyway," said Alice, but she had to repeat it because she had her face in the pie now, chasing a slippery crumb. Matthew was not sure whether St Hilda's was sister to the Minster School because of the sisters and brothers in each or whether it was from some other reason he had not worked out yet. Alice gave him the plate, licked quite clean.

"I have to go," he said. "I expect it's that rhyme." He was still talking about St Hilda's, and Alice knew perfectly well what he meant, but it seemed to her that there were things a younger brother ought not to know about.

"What rhyme?" she said. "I don't know any rhyme, and if I did I wouldn't care, except it's true."

Then Grandpa was calling for Matthew, because both of them had to leave long before the service, one to practise, the other to see to something in the Minster library.

Alice went with them. She and Grandpa conducted Matthew between them along the quiet dull streets of the city, where all the shops were shut and no one else walked and hardly a car came. Matthew thought it was creepy. Grandpa thought, historically, that the city would have been silent like this after a great plague. Alice thought about

St Hilda's. She could remember being near one of the Minster doors a long time ago, with her friend Raddy, and shouting the rhyme at the St Hilda girls as they went in to Evensong. The girls had taken no notice at all, and the Minster door had closed behind them. Raddy and Alice had shouted half the rhyme again after them, the first two lines about green underwear which was true and not very remarkable in a school uniform; but they had each decided not to speak the last two lines, which were only disgusting. Then they had walked off in different directions and not spoken to each other for about two months, and not mentioned St Hilda's since.

Matthew had gone to the Minster School round that time, after passing a difficult exam, and being one of six chosen from seventeen boys wanting to go. Everybody was pleased with him. The next thing was that no one asked Alice her opinion, but suddenly this summer she had gone on a Saturday to St Hilda's and been given a lot of sums and reading and writing to do.

The sums were all easy, the other questions were simple. The only difficult thing was how to tell Mum or Dad or anybody that she did not want to go there, didn't want to live in a dormitory, didn't want to walk about the town only on Saturday afternoons in pairs with another St Hilda girl. She had not wanted to belong to St Hilda's, but she had not liked to disappoint Mum and Dad with a wrong decision. So she had answered all the sums with nine hundred and ninety nine, used very childish hand-writing, and put her own name as the answer to everything else. She had not been able to tell anyone, not even Raddy, and no one had said anything. A great deal of sad disappointment had been about, however, at home, and up in Sarrow vicarage.

Alice had to keep saying to herself that she was right in

what she had done, and it was true: she did not want to go to St Hilda's and the simplest way out of it was to fail the exam. But something had been spoilt, and she knew it was her fault and that she should have relied not on being clever enough to fail but on being brave enough to speak out. Each day at home should have been better than it now was. Today, especially, should have been a particularly happy one, with her and Matthew back and everybody glad to see them, and the service in the afternoon belonging to them all. It was not like that in the slightest, because Alice was the odd one out. But she knew she was right. Matthew had wanted to go to his school and he had gone; Alice had not wanted to go to hers and she had not gone. What she had done was what Matthew had done, chosen for herself; but Matthew was praised and she was not.

The three of them went up the slope of the kirkyard, where all the Minster graves were except the notable people buried inside. Some gravestones still stood at the bottom of the bank, and the yard was still used, but near the Minster the stones were laid flat, or as flat as they could be on a hillside. Alice thought that her own thoughts were lying about more or less level and more or less forgotten, like the inscriptions on the flat stones, and people walked across them without understanding the words or reading the name, Alice Eleanor Dyson who departed.

Then they were in the Minster, and all the long quiet strands of the outside air were folded and refolded to fit under the vaults so that silence itself set silence buzzing. Grandpa spoke, and some low part of his voice went treading round among the chairs in the building, and a high part flew against the windows, and all the middle register gave back a series of echoes.

"Run straight home," he said to Alice. "Matthew and I have to go about our respective businesses now," and without having closed the door they had come in at he held it newly open for her to go out.

She went out, and her ears were swept clean of reverberation and her eyes of shadow. She was alone, and peaceful, and was going to be so for the next forty minutes, and then was to be neither of those things again for a long time.

The Minster clock banged out the chimes of quarter past three. Alice stepped along a bit to see that the chimes and the time agreed, because it was not always so, and put her watch to agree with the hands. Then she set off down the grassy hillside over the carved stones, directly towards the little hill called Eyell. It was plainly in sight, and she wondered again why she had not seen it before. It stood right against the school playground, where she had been an infant, a middle, and a junior before leaving for the Comprehensive school.

She went to it. There are often pieces of the world that get missed, and that was the thing that had happened here. The Eyell itself she already knew about in some sort of way, but the road to it was different. She thought at first the path must be across the school yard, but as she walked across the kirkyard, first over flat stones and then among standing ones, she began to remember that along one side of the school there was a narrow alley, or ginnel, or what was sometimes called a wynd, and that was the way through. The Eyell stood beyond the ginnel, which was why no one had climbed out of the school and on to it.

The ginnel did not lead to it. All it did was lead her round, and she came out in Eye Street, and at the end of that she turned left and came up to the bulk meat shop. Next to that was a field, with a small horse in it, so drooped she could not tell which end was which. She hopped up on the wall, straddled a barbed wire fence, got the leg join of her tights caught on a barb, unhitched herself, and was in the field.

The little horse moved a few steps backwards or forwards. No one else moved. Nothing else was taking place anywhere about.

The way up the Eyell was over another barbed wire fence, but this one had fallen down and was no problem. There was nothing to hinder her walking straight up to the top but a few strands of bramble, and the steepness itself, and perhaps a slipperiness from the fallen dry leaves of the little beech trees growing there. The lower ones still had their leaves brown and dry, but the upper ones were bare.

She walked up to the pointy top that stood halfway up the last trees and looked out. Her first look was towards Sarrow Hill, to where she had been that morning. She thought she could pick out the vicarage. Next she looked towards the most obvious thing, the Minster. Between her and it there was nothing; that is, the view was clear. There was the ground between, that had in it an overgrown orchard and a wall and then the road and the kirkyard, but the space of air was clear, and Minster and Eyell looked at one another very straight.

The rest of the view was roofs, apart from the field to one side, but that had roofs beyond as well as the double-ended horse in it.

That is that, Alice thought. Another empty hill climbed today, and she chiefly felt hungry from missing most of lunch. She looked at her watch and found half an hour left on it, and thought she would stay where she was for a time. She felt safe from all visitations: no one knew where she was.

But where she was had become known, and there was a visitation.

For the time being nothing happened. She continued to

stand on the hill top, out of the world's view. She saw people begin to come to the Minster, in particular the column of choirboys going up the steps on their way to practise: Matthew had been there very early.

Alice stood for some time watching and listening, but she was only listening for someone to call her and discover her, and she was surprised to find the chimes of the half hour coming across to her and nearly finished before she began to hear them. But there was no hurry yet.

She became bored with standing on two feet and shifted her weight to one. It was too late to go home now before going to the Minster again, but too early to go to the Minster. Some other distant clock rang the half hour, clear of the Minster bell, and much gentler, but filling the air more and almost, it seemed, filling the ground below her too.

Then she looked for something to sit on, and found, right at the top of the Eyell, a round stone resting on the earth and showing through a little drift of leaves. It was ready to sit on, and she sat on it. She was glad she had, because the next to arrive at the Minster, in another long queue, were the girls of St Hilda's. Alice felt invisible, almost invisible enough to shout out the rhyme: "St HildAH's, lah-di-dahs, Wear green knickers and green bras", but not quite bold enough to do more than whisper it to herself. The next two lines she allowed not to be thought of because when they came to mind she blushed; and that, she thought, would make her completely visible.

She crouched down a little lower. The St Hilda girls went in, in their green uniforms. The next people to show by the door puzzled her for a moment, until she realized they were Mum and Dad: the odd thing had been the square box one of them was carrying, but that of course was the suitcase with Grandpa's robes in. For a moment after she knew who it was Alice thought she had to hurry away, until she recollected that they must have come up early to bring the suitcase in good time. The thought of having forgotten the time made her stand up, and when she did she found her foot sinking into the ground beside the stone, on the south side.

It was not the ground it had gone into but the little fill of this year's leaves and last year's fibrous remains. She took her foot out without much curiosity and pulled a few strands of old vegetation from the patterned weave of her tights. She saw the space her foot had been in, and that the stone she had been sitting on was not the small boulder lying on the surface that she thought it had been. It went much deeper than that: she could see further than her foot had gone, about an arm's length into the ground. She squatted down and ran her hand down the stone, because it reminded her of some other stone she had seen and she thought she might decipher what looked like carving on it.

There were certainly lumps standing out and dents going in, but a hand cannot read without practice. But it could read, and understand, quite a deep hole with a squared-off edge, and it could go in quite readily.

She thought it was a snake at first, or something less than a snake, a slow-worm; something harmless. Her arm thought of pulling itself away and she did not let it: she was not afraid of little English serpents, and only thought of slow-worms. She held on and pulled gently.

It was no snake. It was fingers and a thumb, holding on to her fingers and thumb and pulling, and she pulled too and knew it was impossible, but her own hand was still being held by another one, dry and rough, and with a ring on one of the fingers.

Her hand was released and she stood up. She thought there was a scream dying in the distance and it must be her own. She did not wait to reckon but turned round and round again and went down the side of the little hill and plunged out into the little field where the horse was. She held her hand away from herself, not daring to look at it. She felt that other hand upon it still and thought it might be there.

She ran across the field towards the Minster, not going back the way she had come, not knowing where she was heading, only that it was away from the Eyell.

"I yell," she said, because her throat had to say something. "Perhaps that's what it means." Then she looked at her hand.

It was her hand, nothing more. It was streaked a little with the substance of the hill, but it was dry and undamaged. She could still feel, though, the pressure of those other fingers.

She was still hastening from that place. The field ended at a high brick wall, and she had to go along and along among the ivy-grown trees to find a way beyond it. She found an ornamental gate with the road beyond and spent a horrible age climbing it and surmounting the spikes on its top.

At last she was down in the road, feeling hot and cold and dirty, and her hand still haunted by what had held it. And now the Minster clock began the chimes of the fourth quarter and she had to hurry again. There was not time to go round to the usual door. She hurried up the north side of the Minster and in at the north door, out of the closing day into the total dark of the inner porch and then into the grainy twilight of the building itself.

She came into incredible noises that she could not sort out and understand. The organ was playing but there were other echoes, and then something that was not an echo but a thing itself. Someone was screaming.

There was the ghostly sight of the choirboys and men

going in to the choir, out of dimness into a hidden light, taking no notice of the howling scream that kept coming. And beyond them, in the shadows at the far side of the building, other people were moving. Dad and Mum were going out of the building, and Dad was carrying Matthew and Matthew was struggling, and the screams were his.

Alice slipped back out of the Minster. She was very conscious of taking her hand with her, as if it were a slightly separate being. She did not want to take it with her because it carried with it the reminiscence of that other hand, and if she could have left both she would. She walked off round the Minster and caught up to Mum and Dad and Matthew in the kirkyard. Matthew was walking now, and sobbing.

"One of the others played some senseless trick on him," said Mum.

"There's some gaumless youths in that lot you wouldn't expect," said Dad, speaking in a very local manner indeed.

"What about the putting in?" said Alice, coming forward and taking Matthew's hand.

It was a shock to her, even though she had begun to do it, to find a real hand gripping her own. She heard and felt her mouth smack open with the surprise of it. But to Matthew it was more than startling: it was terrifying. He held for a second, perhaps, and then pulled his hand away and shrieked, something more than screaming.

"Oh my God," said Mum. "It's a fit."

"No," said Alice, but she was hardly able to speak, because she was full of terror as well as sympathy. She could not draw breath either, because everything was choking her; and she could not look at anything but her hand, which had begun to forget and now had remembered again.

"It's mischief," said Dad. "Laiking on at summat, these two," and he had his belt off in a moment.

"Ken," said Mum, but Dad was taking no notice: he was

going to stop Matthew from shrieking, and prevent Alice from screaming, which she looked to him ready to do.

"I ken some things else," he said, and he laid a smart crack across Alice's rump, and another down Matthew's back. "Now," he said, "say on, if you want, and less of the bauling."

"I don't know anything about him," said Alice, meaning Matthew, who was now quiet, and down whose solemn round face there now ran two silent streams of tears. Alice closed her teeth together tight to prevent that happening to her.

"Something took hold of my hand," said Matthew. "In the vestry, just when the others had gone out. Like a hand."

"I should take my belt in there," said Dad, nodding towards the Minster. But he was putting the belt on again.

"It wasn't their hand," said Matthew. "They weren't there."

Mum and Dad then looked at Alice, and it was plain that they were wondering where she had been and whether it was in the vestry. She shook her head, not wanting to open her mouth.

"It was an old person," said Matthew. "In the wall at the back of the cupboards. All knobbly, with a ring on."

"Dry," said Alice, able to say one word, and then closing up again in case of tears.

"You leave it alone," said Dad. "It's them singing lads, and I'd sing 'em; there'd be an anthem or two, holy holy holy. And what about you, Miss?"

But there was nothing Alice could say. Her story was just the same, in some horrible and unbelievable way. Matthew could tell his, and not be believed, or could only be thought mistaken. But there was nothing Alice could say because only the first telling counted. She had no way of speaking, no way of telling anyone at all.

"We'll not get to the bottom of this," said Mum.

"I would, happen," said Dad. But they meant different things.

"We'll go home," said Mum.

"I'll be banker, and we'll play Monopoly," said Alice, and they did for a time, until the choir bus came round for Matthew. But in each throw of the dice, each payment of Bank Error in Your Favour, there was for both of them the feeling that another hand was nearby, its token not a battleship or racing car but a ring.

3

ALICE AND RADDY had different instructions about the route to school. They had to start at different houses, naturally, but both of them went along Kirk Alley. Then each was supposed to go a different way again, ending at the same school. Quite often they did go the ways they had been told, but since they often met in Kirk Alley, or caught up with one another, it was then difficult to part at the end and go round different sides of the Market Place.

Alice saw Raddy's plumpish little shape ahead of her, and knew her by that and by the red hair that hung down her back, not well brushed and hardly ever combed. But there were eleven children in that family, so seeing to them all before school could not be easy.

"I'm last," said Raddy, meaning that all the older ones still going to school, Joe, Ruthy, Maud, Nell and Ted were somewhere in front.

"I'm first and last," said Alice, wishing that she too had many ahead of her going along the town streets, and more younger ones at home going to another school.

"Well, don't rush on so, daftie," said Raddy. "I'd be with them if I wanted."

Alice looked back at the Minster clock on the west tower. The time was still only just after half past eight, so she had to agree there was not much need to hurry; but she would have liked to catch up with Raddy's family and belong to it for a few streets. She could not join without Raddy, though, and Raddy was in a separating mood.

"Wait if you like," said Alice. "But don't look in that shop window all morning either, daftie. They don't sell real wood."

"I see plenty of them," said Raddy. She meant brothers and sisters, not shops selling artificial boards. "You can catch up to them if you want."

"If you've only got one," said Alice, "then you haven't got time to like him because of all the time you spend not liking him."

"I can spread it out a bit," said Raddy. "But then so can me Mam, and I don't get any notice taken."

"Well, nor do I," said Alice. "It's just the same."

"Specially today," said Raddy, "when our kid's got a rash. He thinks he's allergic to beer."

"You should give him milk," said Alice.

Raddy laughed then, which made her look pretty. Until now she had looked sulky and ugly.

"Our kid's the biggest one," she said. "The one that builds houses. We aren't posh; we say it like that."

Now she was cheerful she would move on towards the Market Place. They had the choice of going together one way or the other, or of parting and going separately. Alice had often thought that they should part and each go the other's way, but she had an idea they might come to school as each other, and while she sometimes thought that would be a good way of gaining a family for herself it might not be fair on Raddy. And of course walking along a particular path did not change things in that way, she was sure.

She was wrong about that, in fact: walking along the right

path and to the right places was going to become very important in a few months' time.

But for now, and quite unimportantly, they went Raddy's way, down the south side of the Market Place and over into Westgate. Alice put this journey right with her conscience by going in her mind along her own route, up the east side of the Market, along North Street, and up another road. She had to imagine it very strongly or it wouldn't work at all. And on top of that she had to imagine things that did not exist at all. Raddy did not have the same sort of imagination, and sometimes thought Alice was being annoying, though at other times she was ready to be amused.

Alice's imagination became very vivid outside the Corner Café, which was just where she would have crossed North Street if she had gone the other way. She looked to right and left along the imaginary North Street and found it very dull and empty and safe, with not even a dog walking in it. However, the real pavement of Westgate was being washed by a girl with a bucket and a broom, so Alice's mind started to pour with rain and the road to flood. There was no way across the next fifty feet, and she could not get the rain to stop or the road to unflood.

"If I could have got that dog," she said, "it would be drowned by now."

Raddy walked on. She sank into the water, except for a few strands of hair that floated on top, and was carried to the far bank. "You're too fond," she said, meaning Alice was too foolish. But nothing stopped the rain until the girl with the water slopped some close to her, and at that touch the flood dried up and it was a mild dry day in Westgate. She waded the river, but it sank away as she trod it; the water was not happening any longer: her imagination had dried up with the water.

"Folks were looking at you," said Raddy.

"I was drowning," said Alice.

"You're getting more daft," said Raddy. "You weren't like it before; it's come on you a bit these last few weeks."

"Oh well, I'll race you to school," said Alice, changing out of that subject for now, because the last few weeks which had certainly brought on the actions Raddy complained of were not ready for discussion yet.

"We'd best hurry," said Raddy, starting off straight away at full speed. Alice gently jogged and came up with her two hundred metres up the road. Raddy was holding her side.

"Stitch?" said Alice.

"A darn," said Raddy. "Patchwork, maybe." She touched her toes twice, but couldn't do it without bending her knees.

Alice won the race. "You were pretending to be a camel," said Raddy. "That's cheating."

Alice had to share a hymn book at assembly. She could not share it with Raddy, who did not come in until after the hymn and the prayer. She was glad not to share it with Raddy, because she was almost bound to dislike the sharer's hand, which was much too close to her own, and sometimes touched it. The hand that had held hers on the Eyell some week or two earlier had not gone quite away. Every so often she would be aware that something she could no longer feel still had hold of her; and just as often she would feel it gripping her fingers, usually because someone was actually touching her, but a certain number of times when no one was there. The hand was not letting go.

So sharing a book was uncomfortable. To get away from the realness of that hand Alice was having to invent other things that might become just as real in memory. The road that morning, turning to a river, was one of the things she was trying. She had not wanted to drown in it, but she had wanted to be able to remember the flood against her legs, wet and pushing, wanted her shoes to fill with water and her sock to pull away from the hollow place at the back of her ankles in the way wet socks do. If she could make some invented fancy feel quite real in memory then she would know that the hand had been an invented fancy too and did not have to be real. She kept hoping that her mind would realize that she had invented her own experience after hearing what had happened to Matthew, putting what he had felt against her own mind and skin. But many trials, tiresome at home and to people like Raddy, had still not brought her anything like it. The hand she wanted to think of as fancy insisted on staying real, like day and night or porridge or the wood in the yard at home, or arithmetic.

There was a Physical Education period in the gym. Alice was standing on one end of the horse and helping other people up and over. She had to put down a hand ready for the oncoming person to take if he or she liked; lift, and let go, regain her balance as she turned for the next; and she was sure she did more work than anyone else. Not everyone took the offered hand, but Raddy was one that needed a hike up.

She had, as usual, started off at full speed from the end of the room, and by the time she was at the springboard she had slowed down and needed a good pull. Alice's hand was there, and Raddy went for it, grinned, and began to come up.

But there came to Alice what often did come, a sense that the hand in hers was the wrong one, not Raddy's, but that from the Eyell. Or, and she was not sure, perhaps she did not take Raddy's hand at all, only the other one. That feeling had already caused Alice to drop a plate that week through finding some extra substance inside the tea-towel.

So now Raddy's hand became that other hand; there was the same grip and pull, and the hard existence of a ring on one of the fingers just as she had experienced it that Sunday more than a fortnight since. One hand or the other let go; Alice did not know which it was, her or the other. Raddy went on climbing with her feet, which she should not have been doing anyway, and started falling with her arms, and flopped down on her back on the springboard.

"Radigund Larkman," said Miss Flowers, "are you all right? Get down, Alice Dyson."

Alice got down. No one laughed at Raddy's full name, because if they did there was Ted, who was nearly eighteen, to reckon with, as well as Nell, Maud, Ruthy and Joe.

"She's been thinking she's a dromedary all morning," said Raddy, sitting up.

"Concussed," said Miss Flowers. "That's certain."

"Just me backside," said Raddy, rubbing it; and the affair was over for her. She went back and took another jump, had a passing push from Miss Flowers, and came over pink and smiling.

"Sorry about that," said Alice in the cloakroom after the lesson.

"I never got hold at all," said Raddy. "I went for a sixer, didn't I?"

"I dropped you," said Alice, remembering all the brains and livers and other belongings that had scattered on the floor and the springboard. Remembering as well as she could what had not happened, so that remembering what hadn't happened would seem more likely.

"It'd take more than you to drop me," said Raddy.

But Alice knew what had happened. It was no use inventing a fancy along that road, because it went through the very thing she was trying to make into a fancy. She forgot about the brains and liver, but very annoyingly they wouldn't go away. She was in a half and half state about what was going on in her mind until the end of school, long after Raddy had forgotten about being dropped.

Miss Flowers, coming out of the school gate as Raddy and Alice went out, slowed her bicycle, which she rode for health and vigour, and asked: "Are you all right, Radigund?"

"Eh?" said Raddy. "I wasn't doing owt. Oh, that; I'm grand. It's her that's all thumbs," and she nodded at Alice.

Miss Flowers nodded too, meaning that she had understood the message and was content with it, and rode on.

"She want to see my bruise or something?" said Raddy. "Chance would be a fine thing."

But Alice was thinking of a hand all thumbs. It might be horrible in real life, but in life less than real it might only be amusing.

"It's a different world," she said.

"It is that," said Raddy. "Get the other side of the gate and you think it's Christmas."

Then they each had their own thoughts for a time. Raddy's were clear, and about food, so they went back Alice's way through the town because that led past a bakery where food could be smelt, but Raddy's way only went past the Corner Café where the food could only be seen and not enjoyed at all. Alice's thoughts stayed with the comforting idea that she might succeed if she tried not to think of different things about the hand, but merely tried to forget it. However you can't not think of something; it always comes back. So for the time being she had an unreal thing with a real memory. Yet there was still that deep certainty that it had been there and still was.

The pair of them took an endless time to get home that afternoon. They were so long getting to Kirk Alley and through it to the Minster that Alice waited under the arches of the west end, where the big doors were, for the choir minibus to come to the five o'clock service.

Raddy waited too for a while. She read the notices by the light of the street lamp that had been paler than the day when they got here and had now hardened yellow as the light was sucked from the sky.

"It's a great copy," she said, as she read. "Your church is named after our church."

"Have you got a Minster too?" said Alice.

"That's what it is, not what it's called," said Raddy. "It's called St Cuthbert and St Peter, and ours is St Cuthbert all by himself." And she pointed out her own church down below, the Roman Catholic one with its two small towers lifted up in a sort of praying state.

"Lots of people have the same names," said Alice. "So they could be two different saints, the same as there might be two people called Alice."

"Just name me one," said Raddy.

"Or there might be two churches like cousins named after one uncle."

"That would be daft," said Raddy. "Churches are girls."

She went home. Alice waited for the minibus, but the choir had its own rules about who sang on any particular day and Matthew was not with the singers. The boys filed in and Alice went home.

"You're good and late," said Mum, who was already in from the office in the woodyard. "You don't want to be wandering about town alone at dusk."

"I was with Raddy," said Alice.

"Raddy," said Mum. "I've heard of Raddy plenty of

times but I've never seen her. I'm sure sometimes she's a figment of your imagination; there isn't such a person."

"There might not be," said Alice. "There might not," and she was pleased with the thought that someone so real could be so imaginary. Perhaps the hand could be imaginary too.

4

ALICE STOOD ON a patch of the last sunlight to touch the
ground. It was the late light of the end of the day and it
was coming uphill and only touched the ground because
the cobbles sloped down the hill. She was arguing with
Raddy, who stood a little way off towards the sunset so
that red light came up her back and seemed to shine
through her knees and make them pink, and get into her
hair and make it scarlet.

"I'm not allowed in," said Raddy.

"Everyone is," said Alice. She saw that the sunlight
below her feet was no longer penetrating to the mortar
between the cobbles; the little dusty valleys were darkening.

"No," said Raddy. "It's against religion. And I'm cold,
so I's off home."

"The Minster isn't religious," said Alice.

"That's why, then," said Raddy. Then she altered her
shape a little in some way that was difficult to see, with all
the sunlight so bright but cold behind her. Alice saw her
getting smaller and smaller, and could not make out what
was happening at once, because of the glare. Raddy went
into shadow and Alice saw that she had turned round,
when she altered her shape a little, but had gone on looking
the same from the back as from the front, with pinkish
knees, dark of school uniform coat, and overflowing blaze

of hair above. The getting smaller had been the walking
away into the eye of the sun.

Alice was ankle-deep in shadow by now but was too blind
to see it: light had blanked out her eyes, and cold had put
its tears in them. She left the place where she was and walked
in at the Minster door.

Here she was in deep, still shadow, and the cold had gone
from the air. The sunlight was coming in at the high
windows and stretching up to the arched roof, holding up
the vault all along the length of the nave. Or perhaps it
was not holding the vault up, but coming down through
it, as if the pillars were trees and the high roof the place
where branches joined and let a noon light down to the
forest.

There was an underbrush of chairs with a clear ride
through, along this length, and beyond that the scattered
rocks of the nave, pulpit and altar.

"I suppose it is religious," said Alice to herself, feeling
the words at her throat. It was, of course, and beyond the
nave altar, beyond the clearing under the great tower, was
a carved cliff with a cave entrance in it, and beyond that
cave was the choir with singing in it. It was the five o'clock
service.

Alice hoped this was the best time to come in and look,
or even touch, the place Matthew had talked about, when
he had been held by the hand that was not his and not
Alice's either. At this time of day all the other people in the
Minster would be in the service, and the vestry was sure to
be open. So Alice thought she would be unnoticed, but not
quite alone; the house would be full of people.

She walked up the centre of the nave. It was as easy as
shopping, or even easier, because there was no traffic and
no weather.

The rocks of the nave altar were railed off like a little

garden: there were two tall candlestick trees, a Towns-woman's Guild banner plant, and a lectern cactus. In one of the set of pews before the altar a hymn book had fallen down open, and lay like a seed packet at the head of a row that was only the crack in the floorboards. Alice thought she would step inside the roped-off garden and pick it up.

But as she lifted the rope by its brass end from the brass hook the music in the choir stopped, and the sunlight switched itself off. It was like a sign. She put the rope back, and a voice started up in the choir, but the sunlight had gone. A grey sky showed at the windows, just bright enough to make patches of light blink where the lead tracery crossed itself. The only other illumination came from the choir, which now seemed to be a cosy house in a dark wood.

Alice stood in this dark wood for a moment or two, like Goldilocks, or since that made her hair colour wrong, like Mousilocks.

The choir began to sing again, first the organ providing the running of deer and the calling of birds, then a deep father bear singing: "Lord, now lettest thou thy servant," followed by a mother bear voice with "depart in peace," and what must be baby bear, but was boys her own age, with "according to thy word."

Alice had arranged in her own mind what she was doing, and where she had to be at each moment. She felt like a burglar, though she was not setting out to steal, only to trespass, to spy out something she alone wished to know.

Her plan moved her along from where she was now, out from the middle of the Minster and along the south side. She had thought it out and knew her next destination. She had to repeat it to herself now, or abandon what she was doing, because, while it was not wicked it was inexplicable;

she would have no way of explaining what she was doing if she was discovered; and no one would have any way of punishing her except by remarking on her newest idiocy.

South choir aisle, she said to herself, banging the words into place in her mind. There were two meanings to the word "choir" inside the Minster. One was the band of men and boys that sang, and the other described the part of the building where they did the singing. She had herself done a childish thing once, when she was a little child, when Mum or Dad had said that they were to sit in the choir and she had assumed they meant among the boys and gone to join them. She had not minded then so much, when they came and took her away, but now the memory seemed a strong part of all the wrong choices she had made and kept making.

Where am I now? she asked herself, and the answer was, In the nave. And if a choir is in a choir then a knave is in a nave.

But soon she was no longer in the nave but crossing a transept, one of those wings spread out from the side of a big church. The south choir aisle was next.

Here she waited until the singing stopped. Next in the service there was the creed, and in saying the creed every person in the choir would turn to the east, all looking away from the west end of the south choir aisle, and it was in those moments, and wondering whether it was legal to move at all while the creed was being said, that Alice was to set foot in the aisle (like Man Friday) and take those few steps to the library door and slip in through it and up the steps to the boys' vestry.

The echo of Amen died away. There was a shuffling as people turned themselves, and Alice moved forward. She saw the candles on the altar glisten, she heard the organ die, she heard beyond the building the traffic pass and repass upon the city roads.

"I believe," said the Precentor, the priest taking the service.

So do I, said Alice, but excuse me for the moment; and she took her few steps to the library door, pushed it open as "heaven and earth" whispered out from the speaking voices in that warm dwelling in the forest, and she was in the warmness of another but a darker place.

She had not thought about dark and light, but now they came to her mind, and it seemed that this part of the building ought to have one or the other, but not what it now showed, both. She was in the dark at the bottom of the steps, but the top of the steps had bright light. The light was disturbing for her. She had been here before, with Grandpa because he worked a lot in the library, looking for things for his books, but she had always been here in daylight. So she had not thought it could be dark here, and she had not thought it could have artificial light, which is what it obviously had.

The creed, the whole of the rest of the Minster, had died away; there was no whisper or suggestion of sound from beyond the door. Alice had a moment of feeling that perhaps she had pulled down all the stonework behind her and was trapped in a cave. Then she walked up the steps, passed the library door, passed another door on the other side she had not seen open before, and went on into the boys' vestry.

Now I am a vest, she said. Then she took it back, through not wanting to be a boy's vest. The vestry was a neat little room with nothing in it but a comb on a shelf, a looking glass, a number of cupboards, and a bench for the boys to sit on while they waited. There was the rather sickish smell of new oak. Alice remembered that she knew something about the oak, and that it had come from Dad's woodyard two or three years before. Until then she had been thinking of a different picture, of old wardrobes standing round the walls, for the boys to hang their jackets in when they put on their cassocks and surplices. That picture had meant she could easily find, somewhere at the back of the furnishing, the hole in a stone that Matthew had put his hand in. But now there were no walls to be seen, only this waxed light oak.

But the light waxed doors of the cupboards had handles and could be pulled open. Alice stepped to the nearest and pulled. There was a little sharp twang as the spring of the catch opened and closed, and the light in the vestry went out. However, light still came in from the doorway, a sort of moving, turning light. Alice stood with the door in her hand and waited to see what would happen next. Nothing did, so she turned and looked at the doorway and through it. She thought she saw a ghost, a white figure moving beyond and going away. She knew almost at once that it was not a ghost, but the impression stayed with her for some time because the crawl of her skin had not finished by the time she realized it was only Mr Beaufort, the Minster organist. She knew what he was doing: he was going down from his organ loft to conduct the choir in an anthem without organ music. He went out of sight. He had economically put out the light as he went by, as if he were in his own house.

Alice smoothed her arms, where the skin had prickled and raised the hairs so that her blouse sleeves were no longer comfortable. Then she turned back to her task. She left the light switched off, because she could still see with the light that came from outside the room. She pulled the cupboard wide open and put her hand in.

Two jackets hung in it, with two caps above them, and on a third hook hung a cassock and surplice. The back of the cupboard was not the stone wall she expected. It was a skin of artificial board, unpainted. She knew it at once, because she was used to knowing about such things, by the feel and by the smell. The board went from side to side and from top to bottom.

She closed the cupboard and went to the next. It was the same, except that it contained one hook with jacket and cap and two with cassock and surplice. The rest of the cupboards were the same, varying only in the clothes they held, and all were lined. There was no stone wall at the back of any of them.

Alice was baffled. She felt that what she had found could not be so; but it was. All she could do now was leave. She stood and thought for a time, and perhaps for too long.

She left, and as she went down the steps again she felt the door at the bottom open in towards her—it pushed air against her face. A prayer being recited came in at the opening, and Mr Beaufort came in with it. Alice was already moving back up the stairs, but she was seen. By the time she was back in the vestry Mr Beaufort had caught up with her.

"What are you doing, young lady?" he said, and Alice wondered that he was able to speak in natural tones while a service was going on. She had nothing to say for herself, however, whether speech was allowed or not.

"You'd better come into the library," he said. "I'm sure you shouldn't be in here."

Alice felt happy enough about that. Like Goldilocks, she would be able to escape as soon as his back was turned.

There were four people in the library. One was Mr Tyle,

the second verger, who was doing an unexpected thing, pouring tea from a red teapot into a number of cups. He was not alone. He had with him an electrician, who was packing his boxes of tools and wire, Mr Kenroyd; there was Canon Bryce, one of the Minster clergy, the librarian; and there was Grandpa, sitting at a table and writing notes from one of the old Minster books.

"Foreign body in vestry," said Mr Beaufort. "Exit, amen, outgoing voluntary."

"Says Private at bottom of steps, on door," said Mr Tyle. "Says Private."

"Why aren't you in church?" said Alice.

"I'm a Baptist," said Mr Kenroyd.

"It isn't our turn," said Canon Bryce.

Grandpa finished his writing, put the cap back on his pen, folded his notebook, closed the book he was taking notes from, and said: "Why are you in church?"

Alice felt herself blushing, going quite red and warm in face and neck and arms. Grandpa looked at her.

"She's my grand-daughter," he said. "She came to say hello to me, didn't you?" And he looked at Alice and meant that he was rescuing her from whatever predicament she was in, as if there were some arrangement between them.

"I've nearly finished," said Grandpa.

"Come in and sit down," said Canon Bryce.

"Take a pew," said Mr Kenroyd, haltering up a bight of wire and stowing it away. Alice sat down on a metal chair that was probably borrowed from the Minster hall. The windows of the library were black against the walls. She was not offered a cup of tea by Mr Tyle.

In a little while the door down below opened once more. There came from within the Minster the prayer the choir sang after they had come out of church, and after that the noise of their feet on the steps. Alice wanted to go out and see whether Matthew was there tonight, to ask him exactly which cupboard he had put his hand in, and where it was, because it seemed not to be in the vestry.

She could not go out. The other verger came in, leading Canon Wright and the Precentor, Mr Blackbushe, who had both been taking the service. While they stood in the way taking off their robes and talking about hospital visiting and some obscure meeting, the boys filed down again from the vestry, the organ finished its outgoing sounds, and any chance of Matthew had gone.

Then Grandpa and Alice were left. He stood up and came over to her. "There's nothing for you here," he said. "Nothing."

"It isn't even proper wood," said Alice. And each of them knew clearly what was being talked about.

"Don't think about it any more," said Grandpa.

But Alice knew she had to think about it, and she hated to be having to, and she hated to disregard Grandpa now that he was talking to her without any trace of authority. So she had to go before she began to cry, hurrying away down the steps and then following Mr Tyle across the dark floors of the Minster to the locked entry by the street, and hearing the key turn and lock her out of that forest with its unexpected rooms.

There is something, she said to herself, in her throat again as she often did; and this time she could not stop the small movements there from spreading up into her face and squeezing out more tears than the cold wind could produce. She went down through the kirkyard understanding and not understanding how it was possible to love Grandpa again in one instant and at the same time determine to disregard what he said. She had to stop among the later graves and whimper behind a tall stone and blow her nose and still not be rid of a lump above the mouth and behind the eyes.

I will find everything, she said, to be a pilgrim. And she was to find.

5

THERE WERE FALLEN sycamore leaves, rolled like gloves, among the beech leaves. Beech leaves are waterproof in look, and hard-wearing, but the sycamores had begun to rub and wear and show their inner threads. Alice crunched both sorts of leaf underfoot in the settled slope of them at the bottom of the Eyell.

She had come this way on a Saturday morning, with a shopping basket to be used at the small Saturday market. It was a journey of no plan that she knew. Coming to this side of the Minster, or really this end of it, had been a matter of chance. But when she found herself by the high wall directly at the bottom of the Eyell she had felt like climbing up it again. She walked along a little further, to the lower wall by the field where the horse was, and came over the wire again. It was an easier step over the wire in denim trousers.

The leaves crumbled noisily. The horse pulled at the short grass. Roundabout otherwise there was quiet, or at any rate no noise belonging to the Eyell; only town noise came distantly.

She set the basket among the leaves and went up the hill alone. She stopped before she came to the top and considered her hand. It was still visited by two things. One was the memory of being held. The other was the certainty that it had not been completely released. Alice calmly considered two more possibilities. One was that something she did not understand had pulled her back here, as if by the hand. The other was that she might have come on purpose to the place again to shake off into that place the remnant of sensation.

However, all four thoughts ran together and became confused. She went on up to the top because of having come half the way.

She was a little disappointed as she went up to find that no strange feelings of any sort hung round the top. It was a place without any particular sensation for hand or mind; in fact she could think it had less about it than most places because it was rather smaller, dropping away so steeply all round, with no flatness at the summit, but no sharpness either. It was a little restricted in its effect.

She stood on the stone again and turned about, looking all round her: across the field, across the road to further fields and the railway line, towards Eye Street that looked blindly back with toilet and wash-house windows, and towards the Minster, the fourth direction, looking back with its huge east window, blind again as a toilet window.

God is watching me, her throat said. Sitting there, said the throat in an irreverent way.

"I'm not saying this," said Alice, aloud, alarmed by the independence of her larynx, smiling towards the Minster. Then she turned her back on it and once more put her right foot down in the gap between the stone and the earth heaped against it. She pulled it out again. To have something hold her hand was better than having something come out and hold her ankle: that would make her helpless; but a hand can be moved, looked at, comforted, spoken to.

She went on having a temptation to put her foot in the same place, but she thought that the part of her listening to the idea, or creating it, was as silly as her throat, and not something she could be quite responsible for, or keep in order, quite.

She knelt, aware of being somewhere between right and wrong, and ran her hand down the stone a little way. Not very far into the gap. Then she knew it was not between right and wrong but between sense and nonsense, and to go any further was nonsense; she knew she could not bear to find that grip in the stone again.

All the same, she had now to know more about the stone, she had to come closer to the place where the hand had been.

It cost her no thought to start digging like a rabbit, from the top of the Eyell down, but not on the side where the hand had been. She chose the other side, if it was choosing that she had done.

The rabbit digging cleared away leaves and then had to stop because the ground below was full of little roots and thorns and angular pebbles. A root came, and a spiky twig, and that was all. Fingers had to dig in a more careful way.

The first few handfuls went down the hill. Alice thought that was wasteful, somehow, and began to heap the rest of the spoil a little to one side. Since the hill had no flat place on it she still lost the material down the slope, clattering on to her feet and pattering down among the leaves.

She was digging against the large stone, and that made the work easier. There was a gap that had been large enough for her foot on the other side, and on this side too there was one, large enough only for fingers, but giving her something to get them into so that she could pull. She was soon beyond roots and into the chips of rock and shaly earth. She hauled and held and hauled and held until she had pulled away fifteen centimetres of hillside the width of the large stone, about sixty centimetres. Then she stopped to move her feet and clear them of the dusty cold earth that had rained down on them. She had begun to scratch the backs of her fingers, particularly the nails.

She went on. She found she was working more slowly now, because the hill widened quite fast as it became lower. She was half crouched, half leaning on the slope. She came upon a larger piece of rock and took it with both hands and heaved it from its place. Her attention wandered from its balanced mass at the moment when she had it upright, because she had disturbed several shining insects and two or three well-tied worms. The neglected stone ran down the bank and clipped both her ankles as it went, so that she had to forget everything else, worms and beetles and the whole world, for a time, and soothe bruised bone. The small craggy boulder she had dug out went hopping down the hill and sighed into the bank of leaves.

The world came back, spreading from ankles outwards. It was not particularly the world of the Eyell any more, because that had given her a hint about leaving it alone, but the world in which she was on the way to the Saturday morning market with a shopping basket. But before hobbling down the hill she turned (since she had had to sit down on the hillside to nurse herself) and looked at the excavation she had made.

She had slid down the hill a little. Her eye was exactly at the level of the bottom of the step she had made. At the back of the step was the great stone, showing its top and two edges in a square. The bottom of this square was a carving like the thick architrave of a door, the framework that surrounds an opening. Inside this framework there was an opening, taller than it was wide, like a doorway, a finger-span high and half that distance wide.

The opening was dark inside, as if it were curtained with black cloth, as if it were open to darkness only, as if it showed another sort of universe that was there yet could not be noticed. It was something that Alice's eyes could not understand, as if they had got themselves focused wrong and were striving to interpret. It was like looking at a photograph and its negative at the same time, all shape and depth that cannot be seen or understood; it was like the thing that happens when you stare at an object for a long unblinking time and the image goes dark and swirling. But with that a simple movement of the eyes restores the picture; with this appearance there was a continuing.

There was a change, after a long continuing, and instead of the appearance being black, or darkness, it became light, though not white; it was only not darkness any more. But it was no easier to see or understand, and it was even more a nowhere place, a none thing; it was still without nature.

Then for a moment that Alice was not sure had happened, that beyond place looked at her with an eye. But it must have happened, because Alice could see in it the shine of eye, and the clear oblong of the opening through which it looked and her own diminished and globed reflection with the sky behind her. The opening became without light again; nothing was there.

She put her hand forward to touch, but it was like trying to make herself touch a spider: something beyond her mind would not let the muscles work. She could not touch with her own flesh. Instead she took a small pebble and put her hand forward with that. Again courage failed. She flipped the stone forward instead, as if it were a glass alley, balancing it on her fore-finger and propelling it with her thumb. The stone travelled twenty centimetres, went into the middle of the opening, and bounced back.

Alice thought that a noise now began to come from the darkness, a noise like a tape running slow and fast at the same time. She became alarmed, and began to heap earth back into the hole, and in that way covered it and pushed the sound back. She intended to fill the hole as much as she could, but as soon as the opening in the stone was out of sight she became frightened, which is beyond alarm, at the memory of that other actuality beyond. She was not frightened of the eye she had seen, or that had seen her, but of the mysterious way that it existed at all in that other medium.

She stopped heaping earth and ran down the Eyell, picked up the basket, skipped over the fallen wire at the edge of the hill, and ran out into the field.

Nothing followed. She was alone. Nothing watched from the Eyell. The horse in the field continued to graze without quite revealing which end was which. Alice slowed to a walk. She wanted to stop to examine her ankles, both of which ached, but she waited until she had straddled the barbed wire by the road and jumped down from the wall before looking at the two holes that had worked themselves open in the weave of her tights. She brushed leaves and earth from her trousers and went on to the Market with the list of onions and apples, as if nothing had happened. But her hands were rubbed by the stone she had moved, and the backs of them and the nails were scratched. And still there was the sense of another hand near her own right one, a grip once released and about to grip again. Nothing at the Eyell had pulled that away.

Nothing added, her throat said, nothing taken away. But she, and her throat, and her hand, did not know much about the Eyell yet. There was something to be added, and something to be taken away.

6

"A BLACK EYE," said Mum on Wednesday evening. "You
should never have gone to that school. I don't know what
your grandfather is going to say."

"I didn't get it given on purpose," said Alice. "And I
don't know how you noticed it: I can't see it from this
side."

"If you ever looked in a glass, for any reason, such as
combing your hair, you would," said Mum. "A great lamp-
lighter like that."

"I used to use the mirror . . ."

"Glass," said Mum.

"Glarse," said Alice. She was beginning to have to
decide which way to pronounce words like glass, which at
school and in the town were said short, not quite rhyming
with "rash" or "hassle" and by Mum and others were
said long. "I used to use it to help me tie shoelaces,"
she explained. "It was more like having you to do it
still."

"Give over stemming the subject," said Dad. "How did
you get yourself a blue eye like that?"

"When you were very young," said Mum, changing the
subject herself.

"No history," said Alice, but it was too late. Alice heard
through hands that covered her ears how her infant self had

had a habit of taking the potty to the mirror, or glass, and sitting there smiling.

"History is a branch of Humanities," said Alice. "Not of inhumanities, and you are being inhuman."

"I just wonder what to do for that eye," said Mum.

"You'll do nowt for that," said Dad. "It's set, is that, like an egg. How did you get it, lass?"

"Larse," said Alice; because, after all, if there is a rule then every word should follow it.

The first year at the new school was devoted to Humanities, Alice had been told when she got there. Humanities seemed to be much the same as ordinary schoolwork, however, and had not been difficult to adjust to. Today had brought a lesson on local history. Most of the class, or clarse, knew that history had all happened somewhere else not in this town. Only Alice had known what was coming when she saw Mr Walker put a certain book on his table. She knew what history it was about, and she knew who had written it, and on what shelf there was another copy. But she said nothing when the class was asked whether it had come across it before. She was happy to stay among those silent ones that had never heard of local history.

She was having a dreamy lesson, partly out of knowing all the things Mr Walker said before he said them, and partly from not wanting to remember Grandpa too clearly. Remembering him made her see how badly she arranged her life, and how he had walked into the world years before her and done all the things she could think of doing, like writing a book of local history. That book.

She was not attracted by the proposition that Mr Walker was making, that there was a lot of history lying about and not yet gathered up, and that the class could very well spend its spare time in the coming year finding out about it and making its own book. It was something already completely done, she thought, and neatly printed and bound in the book on the table. She had heard it before, because of Grandpa's way of telling all the facts there were when he could, whether you knew them or not.

She could forgive Mr Walker for telling her, because he had not done it ten times yet. Then she found something she did not know, and could have known. She had never opened the book, though there was a copy at home, so when Mr Walker went to the back of the room with it, lit up the epidiascope, and put the open book in it so that pages of it showed on the screen she was surprised and astonished.

"But I know that," she said, seeing the photograph of a tall stone with a rectangular hole in its side near the top.

"History is all about you," said Mr Walker. "Yes, it's Easter Cross," and he shifted the page a little so that the caption of the picture showed. "Sarrow Cross, that is," he went on, because that was the caption. "I can't always tell what I'm projecting on the machine."

"No, it's . . . no, nothing," said Alice, because what she had seen had clearly been what she had started to dig out of the Eyell last Saturday. She wanted to think about that more before saying anything.

"Easy mistake," said Mr Walker. "I made it myself, didn't I? There are three crosses remaining, Easter, Sarrow, and Lazy, which is the one that appeals to me most, and they're all the same to look at. The fourth one, at Venwath, seems to have fallen down and got lost some time ago. Even in fairly recent historical times there are mysteries cropping up. But look on the map (which took him some time to get right because of putting it on the screen sideways the first time) and you'll see an interesting thing, if someone will lend me two pairs of hands, just two people, thank you."

There was a good deal of fiddling about with the epidia-scope then, and enormous pink hands groped about on the screen for a time. The picture became clear and free of hands, and the interesting thing was on it. Two lengths of string had been laid on the map. One went from Easter Cross to Lazy Cross, and its path took it straight through the Minster.

"Note also that it goes through the little hill called the Eyell," said Mr Walker.

No, forget that, everybody, said Alice's throat. The Eyell is mine.

"And you see that the other string goes from Sarrow Cross, through the Minster again, and to the town boundary just about at Venwath Bridge, which is as you know the new bridge where there used to be a wath, or ford, on the river Ven, which is obviously where the cross must have been."

But, thought Alice, with her mind and not her throat, if three of the crosses are alike and the fourth is missing, then I have found the fourth, and no wonder they buried it because it has funny habits. And she looked at her hand, and remembered that eye and herself in it.

"You don't agree, Alice?" said Mr Walker.

"Well," said Alice, because she had to say something, "you're only guessing about Venwath Cross."

"Not entirely," said Mr Walker. "It has to be on a road, a highway, and it has to be on a boundary of some sort. I know I said the town boundary, but that is the same, I think, as the edge of the Liberty."

Alice thought he was talking sense, though something was wrong. She had already known, and Mr Walker had talked about, the purpose of the Crosses, which were there at the edge of the Liberty of the town, which was a sanctu-ary. In olden times you could run away after a crime and come to the town, and you were safe from pursuit once you had got as far as one of the Crosses.

"Satisfied?" said Mr Walker.

"No," said Alice.

"Feel at liberty to disagree," said Mr Walker. "I shan't mind." He had the epidiascope switched off, and said the historical part was over for now. Somebody wanted to know why the stones were called Crosses when they had no arms. He reminded the questioner of the hole, or socket, in the stone, and said it was a mortice for the arms to fit in, and showed them a mortice joint conveniently loose on the table he was using. He was asked next what crimes people would be saved from, and there was some discussion about that. Not many facts were known, he thought. The only person mentioned in the book was a witch, or sorceress, who had taken refuge in the town and then come into the Market Place and made terrible frightening threats against the town. Before she had finished them a retribution had come upon her and she had fallen down dead, some said struck by God, and others by the Devil, stabbed with an invisible knife in full daylight in front of a crowd of people.

Raddy stood up then. "That's not right," she said.

"The townspeople were pretty glad it happened," said Mr Walker.

"No," said Raddy. "It didn't go off like that at all."

"I'm sorry," said Mr Walker. "I got it from the book."

"It's my grandad's book," said Raddy.

"It's out of the school library," said Mr Walker. "I took it out after lunch."

"I mean it's a book my grandad did," said Raddy.

No it isn't, said Alice's throat, and "No it isn't," she said aloud.

"It is and all," said Raddy, "and he's got it wrong and you don't know."

It was then, turning round to speak to Alice after speaking to Mr Walker, and because she was standing on only one leg with the other tucked under her, that she overbalanced, flung out an arm, and hit Alice on the eye.

"Mother of God, Alice," said Raddy, the loudspeaker on the wall ding-donged, Alice saw the room all colours, and Mr Walker said, coming between them, "Prayer won't save you, but the bell has," and escorted the pair of them to the sick-room, where Alice had to lie down for ten minutes, wasting the break, while Raddy held a clammy cold cloth on her eye.

"He's wrong," said Raddy.

"Hit him, then," said Alice.

"I don't want to hold a clout on his face, ta," said Raddy. "And you're wrong, too, it is my grandad did the book."

Mr Walker had left the book with them for the moment, but it was not to be looked at until the damp cloth was out of the way. However, Alice thought they could look at the outside, which would prove her right.

It proved them both right. The title on the spine was "A History of Cuttesdon" and next below was Joseph Clements, M.A., which was Grandpa.

"That's right," said Raddy. "Not him. He just wrote it; my grandad did it, look, at the bottom there, Gabriel Larkman, Cuttesdon; he printed it."

"This other one's my Grandpa," said Alice. "But don't tell anyone."

"Sounds more like your nana," said Raddy, "with MA written after it."

"He's a vicar," said Alice. "At Sarrow."

"In our church," said Raddy, "you can't be descended from the vicar. It's against religion. But it's funny, we call them all father."

Miss Flowers came in then, looked at the eye, said it

would be a prize one, took away the cloth, and pushed them out of the room. They stood in a corner of the corridor and looked inside the book. The place was marked for them with a slip of paper. Mr Walker had been right: the tale he had told was what was written in the book; he had made no mistake.

"It's better than funny," said Raddy. "It isn't sense. We'll have to go to the shop and look at the other. You remember every word and you'll see I'm right. It wasn't like that."

The loudspeakers chimed again, and lessons began. Raddy took the book to the library on the way, and the afternoon went on. Alice had forgotten about the eye when she got home. But she had had to explain it.

"Raddy Larkman slipped over," she said. "But it's fair, because I dropped her last week."

"Grandpa mightn't be too pleased," said Mum. "He thought you might like to go up to Sarrow on Saturday for tea, go to the Parish Hallowe'en party there, stay the night, and attend the long All Saints' Day service on Sunday morning, and then you can both come home here for lunch."

"It's funny for him to invite me," said Alice. "I don't seem to be right for him these days." But she was having an odd feeling about Grandpa and the invitation, since the little misunderstanding with Raddy, and since, during all the afternoon's lesson she had said nothing about him and disowned him, and then leapt up to defend him, not only against being Raddy's grandad, but really against being wrong as well.

"I think I'd be all right," she said. "I mean I think I'll be good." And she remembered too that they had some understanding in common about something, though she was not sure that it was.

He had known why she was in the vestry that evening;

he had known, and knowing had made him gentle and considerate. But what was it?

Oh, the crowds of things in my mind, said her throat. And she had to go and lean on Mum in the kitchen because it was necessary to giggle quite a lot so that Dad shook his head despairingly.

"I don't know about the black eye," said Mum. "I hope he doesn't mind." Alice looked at herself in a spoon, right way up, wrong way up, and knew it didn't matter: she loved them all now and they would understand everything.

7

MUM CAME IN from the office. She had to do her housekeeping between invoices and her visits to the kitchen were short. Alice had heard her coming and had turned off the television and put her face towards her books again.

"You can make a cake and take it with you this afternoon," said Mum.

"Me?" said Alice. "I'm no good at Home Economics."

"A simple sponge cake," said Mum. "Grandpa likes that, and you can ice it and put some cherries on. But you'll have to run to the shop and get some flour and some caster sugar."

"If we don't tell him about it he won't miss it," said Alice.

Clomp went a cupboard door in the kitchen, clump went a quick foot in the passage, and Mum was in the room. "Get up at once," she said, "I won't have you speaking like that; I won't have you thinking like that. You've only got your own inclinations in mind, never the needs of others, and get up off the floor and wash your face and brush your hair and get a move on, and why have you had the television on during the morning?"

"No," said Alice, "no, no, NO," but Mum was angry now and it was impossible for the time being for Alice to explain that she meant she would make the cake but it was bound to be a failure and it was after the failure that Grandpa wouldn't miss it. But of course being unwashed and un-brushed and having a sticky plate and knife and a coffee mug on the carpet, and the television betraying her by creaking and groaning as it cooled down, were real causes of complaint. Dad came in while this dusting out of wicked-nesses was going on. He stood in the doorway a moment and then went away.

"And now he'll get the invoice wrong," said Mum. "I don't know why I bother. I could just go back to Sarrow and have a peaceful and orderly life."

"I'd send you a sponge cake with escape-apparatus in," said Alice. "But before you go, and if you've finished about my hair and my face and my breakfast, I'll tell you what I meant."

"It sounded to me as if you'd said the sort of thing you usually meant," said Mum.

Alice explained. "Well," said Mum, "that was the only thing wrong, really. The rest is just about the average thing you have to expect with growing children."

"I was a bit dark about turning off the television, too," said Alice. "It really helps me work."

She took the basket to go shopping. Mum reminded her of the last time she went for sugar. "You left a trail all the way from the shop and the packet was empty when it got to the table."

"I remember," said Alice. "Sugar used to be heavy then, and I put it under my arm and it got more and more com-fortable and lighter and lighter. You weren't funny about that, though."

"You were," said Mum. "You were totally mystified. But go now, and if you get back before I'm in from the office wait for me before starting."

Alice was out in the road before she had worked out what that meant, and that the starting referred to the cake, not to the beginning of the journey to get the sugar and flour.

It was a vexing errand. The shop in Eye Street had no caster sugar and no plain white flour. They had everything else in the world, provided it had a pretty packet, but neither of those things. Alice had to find another shop and decided to do so without going up into the town.

The nearest group of shops was down by Venwath Bridge, and here she found what she wanted. However, outside the shop she came across Raddy and Raddy's mother, coming shopping too. Mrs Larkman was a larger size of Raddy, or Raddy was a smaller size of her mother.

"Good morning Alison," said Mrs Larkman.

"Just say hello, like it was you," said Raddy. "She knows you, she's just got the name wrong, haven't you, Ma? It's the same at home, you have to know what she's calling you. She'll say Ruth, or Joe, but it's me she wants. But I knew it was you, Alice, you're ever so much like yourself."

"That's who I am," said Alice. But she wondered, all the same, which of the selves she was at any particular time, because every time you think of something you are changed. A moment before she had been a person in search of a cake; now, seeing Raddy, she recalled the book Raddy had talked about (at the same time as being Alison for Mrs Larkman's benefit); all these things needed slightly different beings to manage themselves.

"Did you get the book?" she said, because Raddy had given the book a promise twice more during the week and still not brought it.

"We'll go and get it," said Raddy. "Ma, we're just off up to the shop."

"Come back with your Dad, Maudie," said Mrs Larkman, but since she talked in a very level way, unlike Raddy, and it was in the middle of a talk about groceries with an acquaintance, it was hardly possible for Alice to tell what she said and to whom.

"All right," said Raddy. "She said I can go. I understand her, you know: it's just habit. Ma, Alice thinks I'm a cheeky cat."

". . . (wouldn't take a pound at that price) so you are (I told him put them back I said) Nell . . ."

"I'm a cheeky cat," said Raddy. "I've lived with them eleven years; I know the meanings. We'll go up the shop and get that book."

Alice got up to the town in spite of careful shopping in other places. If she had known she would have bought the groceries at the top of the hill instead of at the bottom, but it was one of those days that runs backwards as much as it runs forwards, finishing up at about the right place.

"It'll be a good big cake," said Raddy, when they had talked about the contents of Alice's basket.

"I'll only use a little bit out of that," said Alice.

"You never would in our house," said Raddy. "It'd be the lot, twice."

They went along Kirk Alley and into the Market Place, and turned in at the newspaper shop. Alice realized that the name over the shop that had always puzzled her, The Larkman Press, was to do with Raddy's surname, not with some trainer of birds in a cupboard: a press was where Mum kept all the sheets and towels.

"The press is the machinery bit," said Raddy. "I can work it; you just press a button: I think that's what it means."

Ted and Nell Larkman were in the shop. "Now then, our Raddy," said Ted. "Have you come to serve?"

"Na," said Raddy. "We're off through in the back."

Behind the shop there was an office, with a man at the desk writing in ledgers. He was Raddy's father. Alice had not seen him before, but he knew her. Raddy said that of course Alice knew him; but that did not make it so.

"We've come for a book," Raddy said. "I asked you to bring it down but you never did."

"Help yourself," said her father, "but don't mess on. And it's dinner time when we go, so you've to land on down for it. Three reams A4 bond creaml-laid heavyweight seven fifty time at five times two and a half twenty plus eight per cent value added tax get on with it then twenty one sixty they're not going to like this shut the door after you."

"You can see where she gets it from," said Raddy. "They're both like it."

The room beyond the door had the machines in, each one holding black messages written backwards on grey metal.

"They do books and things," said Raddy. "Don't touch anything. They keep all the words in these boxes. You can't see them properly, they're all lying on their sides. That's an R," and she pulled out a square short rod and and pressed it on the palm of her hand and it had written her initial.

"Just a letter, not a word," said Alice. "Where's A?"

"I don't know," said Raddy. "They can't read, printers, you know, so they don't get 'em right in the alphabet. I just know where R is."

The next room again had the books in. It seemed here that printers not only did not know how to read, but had no idea what books were for.

"They should be on shelves," said Alice, which seemed to her one of the purposes of books.

"It won't be so easy," said Raddy. "I know it's here, mind, because me and Steve brought a lot back from home after my grandad died, and it made a lot more room. We never brought the shelves, because Ted made his bed out of them so that he could sleep in long primer."

Alice did not know what that meant. Raddy thought it

meant he could stretch his legs out at last: it was what Ted had told her.

"I'll have to look at every one," said Raddy. "It'll be quicker with two of us."

"Well it won't," said Alice, "because I should have got home by now and made the cake."

"And there's just one of you to notice," said Raddy. "I'll find it, and I'll bring it after dinner, eh?"

"Not long after," said Alice. "I've got to go to Sarrow for afternoon tea and then the Parish Hallowe'en party."

"I'll come right soon," said Raddy. "Don't touch them press-buttons on your way out."

Alice managed not to touch the press-buttons, but she could not help placing a thumb on the shining black un-readable bed of type on one of the machines, and it came out with a remark about Whist and Mrs Jennings, which seemed a plain statement from such a complication of wheels and levers.

"I'll be down directly," said Mr Larkman, "letterpress at four a page folded stapled bundled packed shut the door postage and packing one pound plus tax . . ."

Alice left him.

Kirk Alley, along beside the Minster where the clock rang quarter past twelve, and then the kirkyard. She rubbed Mrs Jennings off her thumb on someone else's tombstone. She was reminded that the same hand still held that other impression from a month ago, not so easily coaxed off on to another person.

At the east end of the Minster the Eyell was the next thing in sight. She went to it. She had an idea, knowing it was stupid, that she had saved a lot of time by not staying with Raddy, so there was some to spare. She knew it was not right, but not everything can be explained. It meant there was only a little time, and all she wanted was a little time. Or perhaps all the Eyell wanted from her was a little time.

The little time before the next striking of the clock is long enough for her to uncover three more sides of the stone, and to see on each side an opening, mere dark dead places, the shadow inside the cleft in the rock. One she does not touch; it is the one where a hand held hers. Another she looks into again, but there is nothing to see. A third she sees and disregards. Before she comes to the fourth she looks about and from its place where it lies on the hill she picks a thin bar of iron, some passing abandoned rubbish. With this metal she digs at the fourth opening.

At the first push there is a little tempting resistance, a satisfaction in having the metal sink in, and she feels the old rust flake off on hard edges. And at the end of the thrust, when her hand has gone as far as it can and the iron has gone as far as it will, the iron quivers as if a weight had dropped away from it. She draws it out, and it comes glistening, and when it comes she feels nothing for herself but all the world round her seems to move, just a little, and just a little, and then is as it was.

She turns away from the stone and walks down among the fallen leaves. They rustle under her feet and they rustle behind her, and she takes up the basket and goes out across the field and to her home.

8

THERE WAS NO one in the house when Alice got there. Mum had been back from the office at least once, though, because the oven was hot and there was a bowl out on the table, and three eggs on the weighing pan of the scales, to weigh the flour and sugar against. Alice put the basket on the table beside the scales and went to look at her homework again, to try and give herself the impression that she had been in quite some time, so that Mum would get the impression too: the shopping had taken far longer than the time either of them had thought likely.

Alice wondered whether she felt quite well. The carpet she was lying on did not seem to be on flat ground; her back seemed to have grown hollow; things round about her seemed a little more distant than they should, and had a difference about them, as if she were two people, one to look at things and another to understand them, and not quite able to agree on the observations. She wondered if she might be going to be sick in about two hours' time, which would give her the opportunity of lunch first.

The school books were meaningless. She had an idea she had forgotten how to read. She closed them and switched on the television again. The set was playing one of those television tricks and flipping over a picture that was always on its edge so she needed a likewise revolving eye to follow it. Turning some of the knobs stopped the sliding but lost the picture, and then there was something she did not care for: the screen began to display the thing she had seen on the Eyell once, neither dark nor light, neither presence nor absence, the showing of something visible only in another place. She turned the set off.

Mum came into the house then. Alice had a very strange feeling that after she had got through the door there was still only the same number of people in the house as there had been before; as if Alice had not been alone. That thought was very uncomfortable, but there was a comforting one with it. Alice realized that her hand was no longer in contact with that other one: nothing held her fingers; no other and hard hand was touching hers, no ring left its memory on the back of her knuckles.

"I've been back twice," said Mum. "You took your time. Oh my goodness, what's this?"

"What you said," said Alice. "Flour and stuff."

Mum was holding the piece of metal Alice had found and used on the Eyell. Alice could remember putting it down, but not what she must have done, placed it in the basket.

"It looked quite strange when I came in," said Mum. "Like a great knife covered in . . . Well, it's not much better as it is. Why have you brought back such a horrible rusty thing, and what is it?"

"I think it's a doll's pram axle," said Alice. "But I think dolly's learned to walk by now," and she took the rod from Mum's hand and dropped it in the kitchen tidy.

Mum rinsed her hands at the tap, looking at the water running over them. "Are you sure?" she said. "You didn't scratch yourself with it, did you?"

"No," said Alice. "It isn't sharp, or anything."

"It looked sharp," said Mum. "Now you wash your hands; you don't know where it's been."

"No," said Alice. "I don't," and she washed her hands. "You didn't get the weights out," she said.

"Not necessary," said Mum. "Don't take the eggs from the scales; you weigh the flour and sugar against them and you don't have to think whether they are small or large eggs. Put them back."

"I am," said Alice. But she was not. She had lifted the eggs down and set them on the table, along the crack so that they would not roll, and it should have been simple to pick them up and put them back, because the eggs were unable to move and hands have no difficulty getting round them: the only difficulty is holding them with the right firmness. But that was not the problem now.

She picked up the middle egg, not the one she intended, but that didn't matter. It was a falling sort of egg and it wanted to be down on the table again, and her hand would not relate to it properly. She put it down, but not at all where she intended it to be, but about a foot away, against the bag of flour, which was now out of the basket and opened by Mum.

"Come on, don't play," said Mum.

"It's one of those going-away eggs," said Alice.

"It should be all right," said Mum. "It's from Sarrow."

But the eggs were not all right by any means. Alice's hand was near them but not able to take hold of them. An egg that has started to get away on something like a draining board is often difficult to catch because it rolls about in parts of a circle, one way and another, twisting and turning. The three eggs now were doing that, on a flat surface; but there was a difference: the table was the thing that seemed to move, and the eggs were the things keeping still. Yet the table was not moving, because Alice could feel it against her side, quite steady. The eggs were still in a triangular arrangement, not moving from that, but each had a differing movement round it, as if the table moved three ways at once. It was the eggs that kept still and everything else that moved.

There was no time to say anything, or do anything. The pattern reversed itself, like a trick drawing, the table was still and the three eggs went away in three directions. One hit hard on the cross bar of the scales, having risen from the table; one went head over heels, small end over large end, to the edge of the table, somersaulted in the air beyond the table, and then dropped to the floor; one egg, that had been standing on the crack, crumbled to a heap of fragments as if it had always been empty.

"Oh, how careless," said Mum. "But you didn't do that."

"I didn't do anything," said Alice, and at the same time as knowing she could not have done anything she was feeling guilty and hoping she would not be found out, and at the same time as that she knew the feeling was nonsense.

The egg in the levers of the scales had squashed and splashed and spread and broken as if it had been thrown. Yolk was all over the wall a metre away, and shell floated on spatters of white across the table. The tumbling egg had gone down to the floor and lay there unharmed and whole. The third egg had left its shell above the table and all the contents had gone down through the crack and sat on the floor as neatly as if the egg had been carefully broken into a saucer.

"What a curious set of accidents," said Mum. She was not so calm as her words suggested.

"I'll try not to do it again," said Alice, because she knew she had done it but had no way of knowing how.

"Oh, you're priceless," said Mum. "You couldn't have

done any of that. It's just a little uncanny, that's all; but there's a perfectly reasonable explanation, of course."

Alice waited to be told, but there was no explanation. Mum began to clean up the mess. "Here," she said, opening the kitchen tidy and dropping in one evacuated egg shell and parts of an exploded one, "take the plastic bag out and drop it in the bin and tell Daddy it's the end of the morning."

Alice screwed the neck of the bag up, when she had lifted it from the tidy. "It's not full," she said.

"I know," said Mum. "There's only that thing you brought in, and it makes me uneasy."

Alice took the bag out and decided not to put it in the bin for now but behind the nearest stack of wood in the yard, beside the pickle smell of drying oak. Then she called Dad in and went into the house herself.

"You both look a bit dowly," said Dad. "Did you have a worse fight again?"

"We cracked a couple of eggs," said Mum. "We didn't mean to, and it wasn't right."

"Where's the omelette, then?" said Dad. "Eh?"

"Now, Ken, we've had a trying time," said Mum.

"I'll read the paper a bit in the front room," said Dad.

"Drawing room," said Mum.

"Happen," said Dad, and crept away.

Raddy came about an hour later. By then lunch had been eaten and tidied out of the way, and the cake was being made. The eggs had behaved themselves this time and were in the basin being beaten, something that takes a long time. There was a machine that would do it, but Mum said the cake was for Grandpa, so do it the hard way this time. Raddy took her turn, though it wasn't what she had come about. Mum was pleased with Raddy for getting her arm round the basin like a housewife, not in the straight-elbow

way that Alice managed. Raddy became pinker and pinker
and liked doing it so much that Alice let her do an extra
turn.

"I'll wait till we eat it and then I'll go home," said Raddy.
Mum explained that it was not to be eaten yet. "Oh," said
Raddy, "we always eat it straight off at our house or there
isn't any left."

When the cake was in the oven Raddy brought out her
book, A History of Cuttesdon. Mum held it and looked at it.
"You needn't have brought this," she said. "We have a
copy in the house, you know, Alice."

"I didn't know," said Alice, which was true if she meant
the slightly different book Raddy had talked about, and not
true if she meant what Mum meant. What a complicated
lie, said Alice's throat; and I'm not even telling it.
"We want to look at this one," and she hurried Raddy
away to her bedroom before Mum heard any more
about it.

"Your Mum's posh and your Dad isn't," said Raddy.
"Mine are both the same and I'm like them. I expect you
come out the same as me, and I'm normal and I don't know
what to do about it, but you can choose."

"I'm trying to be normal," said Alice. She wondered if
being normal meant she would go on feeling as if she would
be sick in about two hours' time.

"Get your book, then," said Raddy. "That's normal if
it's like Mr Walker's." So Alice went and got it, knowing
quite well exactly where it was.

"Nothing," said Mum, after nearly speaking when she
saw what Alice was doing and Alice had said "Mmn?"

Page 136 was where the difference began. In Raddy's
book the next page was 137, which was not very remarkable.
But Alice's copy went straight to 141, which was odd.

"They've been torn out," said Alice. But Raddy knew

how books were made, and how the pages were folded, and she could show that they were all there in Alice's copy and that there were no extras in her copy, because taking out and putting in can't be done without showing.

"We'll tell Mr Walker," said Raddy. "What will your grandad say when he finds out? I don't suppose my grandad wanted to get wrong with him."

"Grandpa would know," said Alice. "Do you think we ought to read your book? Do you think it's all right?"

"I've read it," said Raddy. "It's right."

But Alice knew clearly that Grandpa was in charge of all the things he did, and that nothing about his book would have been done unless he had ordered it. If four pages had been left out of the copy his own daughter, Mum, had, then there was a good reason. But what I hear I needn't say, thought Alice.

They read the four pages. They were headed "The Deed of Blood", and went on to tell a different version of the story about the witch. At a time that was in living memory when the story was first written down, which was again long ago because Grandpa had discovered some pages written in Latin, a wandering woman, reputed to be a sorceress had come to the town. Her arrival had been expected and feared, because she had travelled all over the north of England saying what she was doing, which was bringing the doom of the town to it. She was certainly a sorceress because she had with her a creature (Grandpa disappointingly called it indescribable, so he had not been able to describe it) that was so frightening no one could come near her. But in the end some brave people had got together and set out to trap her as she approached. But they had not been brave enough to act on their own and had got the sheriff of York to make them legal and a posse. So when they came to arrest the witch she had already got as far as one of the town crosses and was safe from them. But she could not go into the town either, because the townspeople would not let her. And of course she had threatened them so much already that she could not frighten them more, and they thought they might as well be dead without her as dead with her.

They could not stop her talking, and they could not stop the horrible creature she had with her. However, nothing seemed to happen to the town, and the people grew quite bold and thought they would burn her at the cross. When they came with their wood the sorceress became very angry and said she would destroy their sanctuary, either now or at some other time. She climbed up on the cross and cursed the town in her name and in the name of the creature, and as she did so a great knife thrust out from the cross and stabbed her to the heart and down she fell, dead.

The book went on to explain how this was the deed of blood that released the creature on the town, and that seemed to be all that Grandpa had had patience to copy out, because he pointed out that the town was still there, hundreds of years later and so he was not going to trouble the reader with the details of the remedy for the creature because it was "manifestly superstitious, even for those times—enough almost for its attachment to the story to indicate that the story itself was a fabrication."

There were then some numbers to indicate where the old manuscripts were, but the girls did not know what they meant.

"Nowt there we couldn't read," said Raddy. "I knew."

"Oh Raddy," said Alice. "The pram axle. I must go and get it." But she could not get up from where she sat on the edge of her bed, because she knew that she would not find a pram axle but a long knife stained with blood, because she had plunged it not into some unknown place but into the heart of a sorceress living long ago and murdered her.

Then Raddy was moving about, and Mum was in the room, and Raddy was holding a pink flannel and saying "I'll bath her head, Mrs Dyson," and putting the cold slightly soapy flannel in Alice's eyes and letting a trickle of water run into her ears, and Alice could do nothing about it.

Raddy went away, and Alice was hot and cold for a time, and then asleep for a little, and woke up when Matthew looked in and was very interested to know whether she had been sick or was going to be, because of the bowl beside the bed, and he wanted to know what the other fellow was like. Alice now felt perfectly well, with no thought of being sick, but Matthew was not making sense until she asked him what he meant about the other fellow. She was not feeling clever enough to guess very hard.

"The one that punched you in the eye," said Matthew. "Or didn't you get to hit him?"

"It was Raddy," said Alice. "She's gone now."

"Is it a real person?" said Matthew. "It sounds like an animal-vegetable."

"It's a girl," said Alice. "She's the one without a black eye, because I didn't get to hit her."

"I expect that's a joke," said Matthew, "because most people haven't got a black eye, so I can't tell which is her."

"Oh shut up," said Alice, because she had not meant to be making jokes. She had just felt too weak to make her words come out right.

"Listen," said Matthew, closing the door and suddenly sitting on the edge of Alice's bed. Alice looked at him and waited to listen, with her mind floating a bit and expecting musical ribs or clockwork heart chiming the hours, or Morse teeth; or perhaps choirboys got squeaky knees from being down on them in services; or perhaps his hair was beginning to rattle. "I'm different today," he said, as she thought of some of the possibilities. "You know when I was going to get put in, and that thing got hold of me? They put some wood on the backs of the cupboards after that."

"Not wood," said Alice. "Hardboard."

"It didn't matter," said Matthew, "but I never told them so they didn't know." Alice waited for him to go on, but he had done one of the things he often did and finished what he was saying by getting to the end without saying it.

"It's going on in your mind," said Alice, meaning he had forgotten to say what he intended.

"No, it was real," said Matthew, who did not know he had forgotten. However, Alice felt sleepy and patient enough to pull him back through his thoughts. She found out what he meant and was not particularly surprised, after all. It had been a waste of time putting hardboard behind the cupboards because the thing that had held his hand was no longer there: it had come out and stayed with him, as something stronger than memory, and he had had the same troubles with it as she had had, and much the same thoughts. Today, just at the beginning of school dinner, it had gone away, and his hand had been alone. Alice knew about that too. Matthew, now he had told her about it, forgot it: after all, he had not been able to remember it quite clearly enough to tell her without being helped along. Alice still could remember distinctly, and knew she would never forget.

Then Matthew had to go, not being allowed to stay after school tea time. Alice stayed where she was, and the day turned dark across her, and she was strangely comfortable where she was, under a rug on her bed with her clothes on, doing nothing.

The house was very quiet under the darkness. She had to get up to go to the toilet, and no one heard her or called out. When she looked from the window she saw Dad over in the office doing paperwork, and Mum's coat was not there. Alice slipped out into the garden to see whether the car was in. The wind dropped a cone of coldness on her as she stepped off the threshold: she was sure the rest of the world was not so cold as her close surroundings.

The car was out, so Mum was out in it. Alice felt cross and abandoned, and had a clearly stupid thought about staying in the cold because of being so neglected: there was not one light on in the house, only the far one of the office. She liked the effect, however, and thought the right word for it was "witching", and the word came easily to her because she was finding again the white plastic kitchen-tidy bag with eggshells in, and the other thing there was some doubt about.

The bag was where she had put it. As she bent down to pick it from its place it grew brighter, which was startling for a very short time, until she knew that a street lamp had come on.

The bag came up feeling empty in her hands; only the crumple of eggshell was inside it now, feeling and sound being the same thing. The other object had gone.

Yet it had not. It had done what sharp objects will do, and gone through the plastic. Now it was standing in the soft earth beside the damp oak and leaning on the biscuity bark. Alice picked it up.

When it was first in her hand it was what she had remembered without having really seen: a knife, streaked with the strings of red blood. Then it was no longer that, but a length of rusty rod, the axle from a doll's pram, very likely, lost in the rains of many years. The knife-like appearance seemed as if it had been a trick of light, and would not come again. But it was what she had seen on the Eyell; it was what Mum had seen in the kitchen; it was there again now.

She dropped the metal down beside the seasoning oak and put the plastic bag in the dustbin. She opened the house door and went back to bed, just as she had been before, having a very strange feeling upon her that it was important not to wish anything at all because some things might come true.

Mum came back soon. She had been up to Grandpa's with the sponge cake and an apology, and stayed to eat the cake with him.

"You could have gone to the Hallowe'en with him," said Alice.

"Do you still want to stay there?" said Mum. "You look a bit wobbly still."

Alice's throat was wanting to explain about slaying a witch, but it even had trouble telling Alice, because for one thing she knew and for another she didn't want to know. You don't want to know about the murder you have committed when it is quite impossible for you to have done it and there is no victim and you weren't there at the time either. It was too much for Alice, who got up, with her rug, and sat by the fire, and too much for her throat, which settled down to feeling sick again but was not going to be.

The throat was quiet after a time, when some bread-and-milk had been sent down through it. Alice went off to bed early, and could hear out in the street children going by and being ghosts and witches. She thought of the party she was missing, and wondered why she had been led to strike that other witch to death. Then she gradually began to understand all that had happened, and she began to see the solution and resolution of it all, coming like a pattern over her and the town, and changing to a flower, and it was all fine sense but only that dream that leads into sleep, which was where she went.

9

"ALL'S SENSE that makes sense," said Dad. He was holding his breakfast cup of tea with both hands, a sign that he was not quite able to argue with the sense he was talking about.

"It certainly won't be bees at this time of year," said Mum. "You know that."

"Happen they don't," said Dad. "What do you think to that?"

"Indigestion," said Mum.

"Bees or rats," said Dad. "There was summat up there the night long."

"Something," said Mum.

"Aye," said Dad. "It weren't nowt."

Mum gave up the grammar struggle for now. "You should have woken me," she said. "You don't need to go looking in the loft, I'm sure: all you need was a spoonful of gripe-water last night. And now, Alice, you don't seem to be dressed, or washed, and I think I'll be in a better temper without either of you in church with me."

"I'll take the gripe-water up there with me," said Dad. "Happen there's a touch of wind in the roof; and then."

"And on a Sunday, too," said Mum.

"Better the day better the deed," said Dad. "It won't be wind up there, mind; it's as still as junket outside and has been all night."

By the time Alice was dressed Dad was up in the roof. The ladder to it stood in the hall and no one could open the front door. Dad knew what he was doing in the roof because he had made it himself. He had made the whole house, in fact, except for the final six months' work, which Mum always said she had done by refusing to come and live in it until it was completely finished.

Alice thought of snakes, of some large and foreign kind, rustling and coiling overhead. Some of the noise now coming out of the roof might have been an enormous swallowing of Dad, but since he went on whistling gently it was unlikely. Alice went to her homework.

She got as far as one word written down, with her pen nib making a noise like a very small snake. Then a visitor came to the door. Alice had to go round the house and surprise her from the side.

It was Raddy. "This is the door I came to before," she said. "I thought it was the one you use."

"We do," said Alice. "It's all bunged up with bees and rats and snakes and bad dreams just now, so you can come in this other way."

But it was not so easy as that. Alice put out a hand to take Raddy's arm, and there was something like an explosion of a small sort, a soft electric shock between them and some light and a little something like steam. Then the stillness of the day, which had been as Dad said, set like junket, lifted itself and shook.

"Oh," said Raddy. "What was that?"

Whatever it was it had gone, and the morning was still again, with the Minster bells still sounding up on the hill like plates sinking and knocking together in a big bowl of water. There was noise inside the house, though, a running clatter with a series of thuds, and then again quiet.

Dad could be heard after that, calling out. "Give over,

Alice," he was saying. "Stop your tricks and pull the bolt back. Come on, that's plenty of daftness, plenty enough."

"I'm not doing anything," said Alice. "He can't hear me from here. We'd better go and see."

But when she and Raddy came to the back door it was shut against them, and locked. They could not get in. And Dad was in the roof still calling out.

"I'm going," said Raddy. "I don't know what happened, and I'm frightened."

"Don't think about it," said Alice.

"I'm not," said Raddy. "I know it; I don't need to think; it's there. Something terrible happened and I don't know what it was."

"I just touched your sleeve," said Alice. "It was just one of those electric shocks. You can get them off a school blouse if you take it off in the dark."

"I know," said Raddy. "It blips your nose and then sucks it. You must have got a week's blouses on to do that. And what's going off in the house, then?"

"I don't know," said Alice.

"We both don't know," said Raddy.

"Nor does he," said Alice, because Dad was still shouting to her. "I think the trap's fallen down and locked itself like the back door, and Mum's gone to church, so there isn't anything I can do."

"We've all been to church," said Raddy.

"I don't see what difference that makes," said Alice. She remembered that remark a number of times later on. But for now she thought of going to get Mum, and realized that the bells had stopped and the service had begun. It was too late for that. "What are we going to do for him?" she said.

"I'm off," said Raddy, and began to walk away. "It's too mysterious for me."

"It's just as mysterious for me," said Alice.

"I'm going out in the road," said Raddy. "It'll be safer. I'll say a prayer."

"No, don't do that," said Alice in a firm voice she was surprised to hear herself using. At the same time her throat seemed to be wanting her to say something different, and her mind couldn't make itself up.

"I'm off," said Raddy, again. This time she went out into the road. Alice followed.

"I can't just stand here in my slippers," she said. "I'm cold."

"We'll go and get our Barney," said Raddy. "If he's up. He goes to church on the way back from the pub, he says."

Fetching Barney took as long as waiting for Mum, but was warmer. At Raddy's house Alice sat by the kitchen range being looked at by a set of smaller Raddy-like children called Freddy, Sissy, and Bobby. Some of the older ones were in another room doing homework, Mrs Larkman was cooking quantity enough for a school, and Raddy was upstairs pulling Barney from his bed. She got him out once and he followed her downstairs in his underpants and had to retreat to bed again when he saw a female stranger in the kitchen.

"Warm my bloody trousers then, Rad," he shouted, throwing them down the stairs. Mrs Larkman, rolling pastry, gave a great shout at his swear word, in much the same way as she spoke at other times, without stopping what she was doing or saying already. But she did follow her shout with a small quick smile towards Alice, to show she was ashamed of Barney or sorry for shouting. Raddy warmed the trousers and took them back to Barney, and he came down in them. Then he had to have a cup of tea and sneeze violently three times. At last he was ready for Raddy to lead him away.

"He'll wake," said Raddy. "I'm his favourite sister."

"He's welcome," said Nell from the next room, and Mrs Larkman slid a remark about Barney being best in a dream into a small but long scolding of Sissy for fingering pastry.

Barney woke up as they went along. "You want the fire brigade," he said, when they had managed to tell him what was wrong.

When they got there he shouted up, "Are you fast, Mr Dyson?"

"I am that," said Dad. "And I've the roof so well stemmed with fibre-glass there isn't any heat coming up, and I'm starved. Who's yonder, anyroad?"

"Barney Larkman," said Barney. "Tha knows, Boniface."

"Oh aye," Dad shouted back from under the tiles. "What'll you do? Can you get in? Where's our little lass?"

"She came on for me," said Barney. "I'd ha' been on sooner, but I were ligging i' bed."

"Get thysen moving," said Dad. "If I's here much longer I'll not bend to come out."

Barney tried both doors. They were both locked.

"Told you," said Raddy.

"Daft not to try," said Barney.

"And what are you doing?" said Mum, coming in from church at that moment, when Barney was shoving firmly at the back door.

Mum was no help. She had only the front door key, and the front door would not open more than one inch. That was enough for them to be able to see the trapdoor shut in the hall and the bolt across.

"Will I lift off a slate or two?" said Barney.

"Put Alice through the toilet window," said Dad.

"I'll put our Rad through," said Barney. "No loss if she goes down the drain." However, Barney went through himself, while Mum held up the window with the yard broom. He went through head first, and as he disappeared within he touched the flush knob and water roared.

"He's gone himself," said Raddy. "We'd best go for Steve; he's the plumber."

Then the back door opened and Barney walked out the right way up. "You'd best come in," he said. "It's a right mess. I'll go and let him down from the loft."

The right mess was every piece of dust that had gathered in fifteen years up in the loft. It had all come down and spread over the whole house.

"This needs Nell and Maud," said Raddy.

"You stay out, you girls," said Mum. "You two men come out of the way too. I'll just vacuum along the hall and the passage and put some paper down, and that's a start. It's just dust; it isn't mud."

"My ma would have screamed," said Raddy.

"Nowt up there, neither, to cap all," said Dad. "I'd plenty of time to look. Just a little old ring. I don't know how that came there. I brought it down, I couldn't tell, it might have been gold."

"Bit of ring solder from a Yorkshire joint in the plumbing," said Barney, and flipped it out into the garden over his shoulder.

"We'll go and spend it's worth, eh lad?" said Dad.

"Yes, you go out," said Mum. "Lunch will be a bit late. Go on, I don't want you."

Mum's tidying up after the occurrence was very severe. Nothing was in the right place all that week. Alice lost her homework completely and found the book on Wednesday in a place she had looked, under the sofa. Mum could not find a bag of flour, and it turned up in a bedroom cupboard, so that she worried in case she was becoming absent-minded, a thing she never truly was. Dad lost a shoe, the left one, and when he found it the right one was missing, and when Mum found that behind the refrigerator Alice was sent to bed because it must have been her doing. Alice was very angry about that on the day it happened, Thursday, but what happened next was not done by her, because Mum was crossly pushing her along to her bedroom and into it at the time. They had got to the door, which was open, and Alice was resisting a bit but they were moving along nevertheless. Mum put the light on, and was about to say some more things about stupid behaviour, when two small objects pinged against the door beside Mum's head and above Alice's, and dropped to the floor. They were two screws, and for a moment it was not clear where they had come from, because above was the obvious place and there was only the ceiling. In a moment it was clear that they had come out of the wall on the other side of the room, where they had held a bracket that in turn held a bookshelf. The bracket swung out from the wall, the shelf tipped, and the books fell down. They did not fall straight down but glided across the floor, ending in a fan shape like a spread of playing cards. Then the shelf somersaulted over them and lay on top of them, and that was quite an unnatural arrangement.

"Oh," said Mum, holding Alice's hand tightly. "I don't think you'd better go in there."

"It's my fault," said Alice. "I was thinking destructive thoughts."

"You don't know words like destructive," said Mum.

"I knew that one," said Alice. And it seemed to her as if she did know what had happened, and had somehow done it, though of course it was not possible. So she was now telling Mum not to be frightened, and was not frightened herself, only a little alarmed at thinking destructive thoughts and then having them come true.

"I'll be careful," she said.

"Get on with you," said Mum. "Go and tell Dad to bring a screwdriver. You can still go to bed for your foolishness."

Alice went for Dad. Her brief understanding that she had made the screws come out and fly across the room and the books fall went away. It was just something that had happened. She sat on her bed and watched him put the screws in again and put the shelf up, then she put the books back and went back to watch television, and Mum decided to say nothing because she was uneasy too.

10

"YOU'VE CHANGED, Alice," said Raddy on one of the mornings of that week.

"No I haven't," said Alice. "I'm not a changing sort of person," because she thought she did what she wanted to do, and while the things she wanted to do would change, the person doing the deciding would not.

"Yes you have," said Raddy. "That's two days this week you've caught up with me before I've got to Kirk Alley, and you don't usually come that way."

"I do what I want," said Alice. She began to feel a little angry with Raddy, and wondered whether to be unkind to her or not. Then she thought she had better explain about the kirkyard, the way she no longer came.

"I was getting dust in my eyes," she said. "It gets very draughty this time of year up there."

"Does it heck," said Raddy. "The air's like curds, you can hardly stir it."

"Not up in the kirkyard," said Alice. "It just looks still because you can't see air, then all the leaves and sand and stuff lifts up."

"O.K., then that isn't a change," said Raddy. "But you have changed."

"No," said Alice.

"There was that time when you had something wrong

with your hand," said Raddy, "like it had something growing on it, moss or lichen, and you were always looking at it
and rubbing it against things."

"It's the only way to get the lichen off," said Alice.

"No, side up," said Raddy, meaning Don't be silly. "And
then you weren't right on Saturday and you did a funny
trick on Sunday, and I don't know what you did in
the prayers bit of assembly yesterday because I don't go
in."

"I didn't do anything," said Alice. "It was one of those
rows of chairs and they weren't hooked together properly
and they all fell over."

"They couldn't," said Raddy.

"They did," said Alice. "It was funny. He said Let us
pray, and all the chairs knelt."

"It's a bit like you these days," said Raddy. "If you don't
mind me saying so. You see, it is a change."

By then they were at the Market Place. Though they
usually stayed together once they had met, today they
separated, Raddy going her way and Alice hers, as if they
hadn't met at all. It seemed to Alice the easiest way of
ending the conversation. She did not want to go on thinking about changes, but at the same time she felt that she
was only acting unchanged and that something was different.
But she could not bring herself to explain to Raddy, or
anyone else, about the Deed of Blood and the slaying of the
witch. She was sure she had done that, and that some other
thing would follow from it; she could feel it shaping her
life ahead, perhaps shaping it now, because nothing is the
same after even an innocent murder.

She walked back with Raddy, however, and they talked
about other things until they came to the end of Kirk Alley,
and then Raddy thought she would like to go through the
kirkyard and taste the wind for herself. She said there could

be no wind, with all the mist settling over the river Ven and the sun going on its way down into a yellow haze and nothing stirring but traffic. A leaf falling from a tree dropped straight and sat on the ground as if it would never move again.

"It won't do it," said Alice.

"It won't do it," said Raddy. "Away then."

At first they were in the common calm of the day. But Alice knew the wind was to blow soon, and it did. "It's up by the Minster walls," she said. "It's high up and it catches it."

"There isn't a breath," said Raddy. Yet there was a breath of wind, not ahead of them by the Minster, but where they were, pushing and buffeting, doing what Alice had said, driving sand and gravel against their legs, dead leaves round their heads, and dust into their eyes.

"See," said Alice, but her mouth filled with a drift of flying matter. Raddy wrinkled up her face, and a stroke of the raging air drove her breath from her body.

"You could run a windmill," said Alice.

"I could run a mile," said Raddy.

"I can't be bothered with it in the morning," said Alice. Since Alice knew the wind was worse by the building they left the path and walked among the tombstones. As they went down the hill the tempest eased, and they were able to stop and wipe muddy tears from their eyes.

"I still think it's you," said Raddy. "Are you practising for a witch?"

"Just Household Economics," said Alice, "like the rest of the year." While she was speaking a thought almost took shape in her mind, but she was not quick enough to catch it. She sorted out what was grit in her nose, what her throat was trying to say to itself (Cry-baby suck-a-thumb, to Raddy, who had a tear like rain on her cheek), but the glimmer of some understanding would not quicken into flame. "Say that again," she asked.

"You answered me," said Raddy. "Are you practising for a witch?"

Nothing came to Alice's mind. The tiny light had gone out; nothing remained.

"Go on," said Raddy. "What's the answer?"

"I don't know," said Alice. "Am I practising for a *whom*?"

"A hooman been?" said Raddy. "I've come the wrong way; I'd better go home," and instead of thinking for a moment and going along the bottom of the kirkyard she turned and ran across it the way they had come, because she had forgotten about the wind. And there was no wind; she ran easily through calm air.

Yet Alice always found the storm blowing, and found its limits in the next three days, taking her course round certain graves in certain directions and keeping away from what blew.

But on Sunday there was no dodging it.

By then the calm weather had sunk into the ground: it could hardly have moved, it was so inert. A wind began to blow on Saturday evening, bringing with it great slaps of rain and taking away for certain the last leaves on all trees. Sunday was a cold and clear day, with the air seeming to magnify and make sharp everything round about.

"It's better than all that closeness," said Dad. "Now, we've nothing out of the way today, have we? Then we'll get ourselves off to the morning service and maybe see Matthew at it in the choir."

"He'll be there," said Mum. "He gave me a list last week, and I think I can read it."

Alice looked at the list, but she had difficulty in knowing which Sunday was meant because they did not have dates, only names like Advent I and Nativity and Epiphany, which were words she knew without having their meanings.

"Give it to me," said Mum. "Yes, he's singing today."

There was a gleam of sunshine when they went out of the door. It silvered all the edges of the wood in the yard as if the drying stacks had been plated. There was another glitter too, at the base of the nearest stack. Alice let her eye stay on it while she walked two paces. The shining thing faded to being the rust of the doll's pram axle. Alice thought she would throw it away the next time she came outside. The wind came thin from the west and splashed drops of rain from the trees. The drops fell on the stone pavement, for a moment becoming its colour, as if the stone had lifted up rather than had something land on it; then the stone was undisturbed again, merely wet.

Mum hesitated a bit with an umbrella, and decided there was not enough rain to make it worth setting up and drying later. They walked round to the kirkyard and entered it.

"I feel a bit funny," said Alice. "I haven't got my shoes on."

"Yes you have," said Dad. "What do you mean?"

"You could have put the black ones on," said Mum. "But those will do."

"I feel ridiculous," said Alice. "I'm not me."

"You're all you've got," said Mum. "Stop being foolish."

Alice came on a bit further, trying to work out what her feeling was. It was dread, she thought, dread of going to church in the Minster, dread and sadness and misery. The feelings were very strong, but she remembered what she had told Raddy, that she had not changed. At the same time she knew that the feelings were not really her own but were being put very close to her so that she thought they were hers.

"Perhaps you don't want to go to church?" she said.

"I certainly do," said Mum.

"And right sharp, too," said Dad. "Away, the wind's rising on us." The wind had grown stronger and begun to flap at them from other directions than the west, lurking among the tombs and graves and making eddies of wet leaves still firm from being in the air.

"I'll try," said Alice. "I'm not wanted to go to church."

"It isn't up to you," said Dad. "By gum, it's more blowy than I thought."

They walked on, Mum and Dad trying to stand upright and take no notice of a little weather, but having to bow to it in order to move, and Alice bowing too and holding back and then holding on to them both and knowing this was the wind she had met before and not changing and not giving in to it and shouting to them both to help her along. Mum was talking back to her, but Alice did not have time to hear what she said; Dad was saying little but what he said seemed not agreeable.

"I am trying," Alice shouted. "Help me."

So they came up through the kirkyard, and Alice knew the storm was only round her and that if she let go and ran away it would follow her a certain distance and then stop and they could go on unhindered, and she knew it was her storm and could do nothing about it but resist it. They came up to the door and the wind tried to turn them away and threw dead leaves and twigs at them, raising them high overhead.

And then they were on the step and inside the building, with the door hurled open before them, so that Alice, and Mum and Dad looking out could see the whirlwind at the entry lift and spin and disperse and a cloud of suspended rubbish, twigs and leaves and scraps of paper, begin to fall down the gentle west wind towards them, because the storm had gone. But when the falling stuff was almost at the ground one last huff scattered it all in on top of them, opened the inner door, and threw the damp mud and dust and splash into the transept.

"Well, that was a sharp do," said Dad. "And you didn't help, miss, with your carrying on."

"If we weren't where we are," said Mum, "well, I don't know, I suppose you're too big for what'd do you most good."

"You don't understand," said Alice. "But it doesn't matter," and she gave Mum a kiss.

"I don't want to understand," said Mum. "Go and get some prayer books."

Alice went to the rack and brought the books, and the music of the organ sang round her, and the tangled rhythms of the bells came down through the fabric of the building, and there was a great peacefulness. There was no more dread and no more sadness and no more misery, because all that had been left outside in the wind and the struggle.

It was plain to her, as well, that there was something real out there that had caused the wind, that had pushed unhappy feelings towards her, and at the same time she knew that her own unchangingness would deal with that, and that inside the Minster there was a safe harbour. But it was not a religious feeling at all; it was like being in a real harbour in an unknown land, where all that mattered was the shelter.

All she felt was that she rested in a place of rest, and went through the service in a dozing fashion and sucked her thumb all through the sermon. Then, coming out of the Minster later it was as if she took some of the safety with her, and they got home without event. It was not until after tea that she knew she had been found again, when, from nowhere, something dropped on the back of her hand while she wrote out the end of her homework. It was a small black dirty-looking ring that looked as if it had been buried a long time. She nearly put it on, but there was still the memory of that hand that had held hers, with its ring. She slipped a pencil through it and dropped it and the pencil into the coke boiler in the kitchen and heard the pencil blaze. She did not know what became of the ring.

"No," she said, wanting something to understand her. There was no reply.

11

"YOU'LL BE LATE for school," said the policeman. "You'd better call back. I'll give you a receipt for now, and I'd just like to hear about it this afternoon."

"Give it to her," said Alice.

"I didn't find it," said Raddy. "She found it."

"Better get it right," said the policeman. "It might be finders keepers, you know."

"I don't want it," said Alice. "I don't want any of them."

The policeman was not very happy about that remark. "I think you'd better talk to one of our police ladies," he said. "If you've got more of these things."

The thing Alice and Raddy had brought in lay on the counter of the police station, silvery and shiny, and silvering and shining upon the dark wood. It was a clean bright ring with a diamond (Alice thought it must be a diamond) raised up on one side of it. It was rather ugly and clumsy, but in the jewel of it lay lights of blue and red, and they were beautiful. Alice had found it lying between two cobbles at the edge of the Market Place. It had winked at her as she walked near it, and she had stopped and stooped and looked at it and been tempted to pick it up and put it on. Then she had stood up and been ready to walk away and disregard it. Raddy had said it looked real, and she had picked it up.

Alice had let her, because she knew if she took it herself she would change, and she was not going to change.

The police station was just the other side of the road, so they had stepped across and put the ring on the counter. Raddy did it, but they were together.

"She's right funny sometimes," said Raddy. "You don't want to listen to her."

"I tell you what," said the policeman, writing in a little book, "I'll ask one of the ladies to come in while I'm making out this receipt, and you talk to her." He considered one of the telephones on his side of the counter and pressed a button on it. A voice crowed back at him and he asked Miss Bennet to come through, and an ordinary young woman came in at once, not in any uniform and not looking official.

"Hello, Yvonne," said Raddy.

"Good morning, Radigund," said Miss Bennet.

"Young ladies found this ring," said the policeman. "Will you talk to them about it while I finish the receipt. I just want the taller one's name for the form."

"That's you," said Raddy. Alice said her name, and, as usually happened, it was written down as Alison.

"So what's the problem, Raddy?" said Miss Bennet.

"Nothing," said Raddy. "She found it, I picked it up, and there it is. Well, there it was," because the policeman had picked the ring up and tied a label to it, with Alice's name (wrong) on the label.

"Alison said something about not wanting that ring or any of the others," said the policeman.

"I see," said Miss Bennet. "Where did you find this one?"

"Simple," said Raddy, and they went outside, across the road, found the crack between the cobbles, and there was the smooth print of the ring in the damp dust.

"And that's all?" said Miss Bennet. "Were there other rings, or anything like that?"

"Nothing," said Raddy, and Alice shook her head. She could see that the police were thinking of jewellery, and she was thinking of rings, and there was a big difference.

"And look," said Raddy, "it's clonking nine on the Town Hall clock and we're late for school."

"Don't worry," said Miss Bennet, "I'll run you along in the police minivan." So they got not just to the school gate but right up to the door.

"Goodbye, thanks, Yvonne," said Raddy when they got out, and she waved the van out of sight. "She's nice; she didn't know whether to be a nun or a policewoman."

"Have we got to go back later?" said Alice.

"Have you got your receipt?" said Raddy. "So you can claim the finders keepers for it when it doesn't belong to anyone."

"Yes," said Alice. But she had already, with her hand in her pocket, crumpled the paper to dusty silk and broken it in pieces. She dropped the pieces in a waste basket during the morning. She did not want it; she did not want the ring; she had meant to walk past it because it had been lying in wait for her, to make her hand like that other hand. She would not change.

Alice had not had time to tell Mum about the ring and the visit to the police station before she found out for herself. Alice was sure she had not been going to say anything in any case.

A car came peering along the road. It had in it a man and a woman and a long-looking St Hilda girl with freckles and a slightly runny nose so that she sniffed every seven seconds. They all got out of the car when it stopped outside the house.

"Grandpa's friends, I suppose," said Mum, who was

quite busy with getting tea ready. "A fine time of day to call."

"It's a bit of a show-off car," said Dad. "More room for engine than for folk. Get shot of them right sharp, will you? I want my tea."

"One's company, two's a crowd, and three's a party," said Mum. "I'll be as quick as I can. I don't know why they've *all* come."

The doorbell rang. Mum closed the kitchen door and went out across the hall. The front door opened and there was some talking. Then the front door closed and Mum came back to the kitchen.

"You soon saw them off," said Dad.

"Hush," said Mum. 'They're still here. It's Alice they want to see, only they call you Alison. You'd better take them in the drawing room."

"Aye, the front room," said Dad. "Have they brought a dog with them? What's that sniffing?"

"Their daughter has a cold," said Mum.

"She looks that sort never without," said Dad. "Go on, Alice, it's you they want."

Alice went out into the hall. She could tell at once that no one there wanted to be at all. The man had had to come because he drove the car, the girl didn't care, Alice wanted her tea, and the woman didn't know what to say.

"I was so upset when I lost it," said the woman. "Wasn't I, Andrea?"

"When you found out you lost it," said the girl.

"It's the same thing," said her mother.

"She's talking about that ring," said the man. "My wife lost it last night some time, and when I went round to the police they said you had handed it in."

"I was so upset, where could it be, I wondered."

"So she's come round to say thank you," said the man.

"I'm Mrs Willis," said the woman. "We live at Osmington, and you must be Alison and this must be Andrea, I mean, it is Andrea. She goes to St Hilda's."

Alice's throat said it knew. She said nothing herself.

"My lovely ring," said Mrs Willis. "I looked everywhere."

Sniff, went Andrea. "She looked everywhere," said Mr Willis, "and I went to the police station this morning and found it and now my wife has come to say thank you."

Alice's throat was thinking about asking them into the front room, and her mind was thinking about asking them into the drawing room, but her mouth did nothing about it. Andrea sniffed; Alice felt she too might have to any moment now.

"We hadn't offered a reward," said Mrs Willis. "We were too upset, weren't we? But if you like to name a charity we'll give something to that, won't we, dear."

"Where would you like it given?" said Mr Willis. "She'll say thank you in a minute, I dare say."

"You must have a favoured charity," said Mrs Willis. Andrea sniffed. Alice wished that the drop of runniness would escape from Andrea's nose, but otherwise her mind was not working.

"None," she said. Then she thought that was not quite good enough, so before the word died away she added a zz sound to it and made it nuns, because she was sure nuns were a charity but police ladies weren't.

"Very well," said Mrs Willis. "We shall ask the Bishop about the Anglican nuns, because we couldn't give to the others, you know. And now we must go."

"I think she's past saying it now," said Mr Willis. "But Osmington isn't so far off, and any week-end you want to visit Andrea and have a ride on a horse, you'll be welcome. Here's my card. You just ring up . . ."

"I was so upset at losing it," said Mrs Willis.

"A different sort of ring," said Mr Willis. "You telephone, and we'll come down for you, won't we, Andrea?"

Andrea gave a despairing desperate sniff but she could not make it a long enough one, and when her lungs were full of air she exploded into an enormous splashy sneeze.

"I'm off," said Mr Willis. "She means thank you, does my wife; but I can't make head or tail of Andrea." Then he opened the door for himself and led them away, Mrs Willis smiling and looking at the gravel path as if she were curious about what kind of carpet it was, in case it was rare; and Andrea mopping her face and hands with a tiny handkerchief with lace edges. Alice watched her clamber into the car and show the world her green underwear.

"What was all that about?" said Mum. "You never said a word."

"I said none," said Alice.

"That would be the same thing even if it was different," said Dad. "Let's get us tea."

"I found that lady's ring this morning," said Alice. "They said they'd come to give something to charity for me."

"More like to have given you pneumonia," said Dad. "Was it the three of them sneezed together? What's that card, the charity?"

"That's them," said Alice. "They said to go up there and ride a horse any week-end."

"Drain those potatoes," said Mum, "and tell me about the lady and the ring."

The next evening there was another visitor, walking this time, and carrying a black and complicated object.

"Breathing apparatus," said Alice.

"A camera," said Dad. "That on top is his flashlight thing."

"You go and see to him, Ken," said Mum. "I'm making a white sauce and I won't stop."

Dad went to the door and came back again. "It's for Alice again," he said.

"I wish you'd arrange your social life a bit more conveniently," said Mum. But what she meant was that she could not understand why anyone would want to come to see Alice and that she was going to find out all about it first, this time. "He'll have to come in," she said. "We aren't going out."

"I'm from the Gazette," said the man. "You must be Alison Dyson."

"No," said Alice, but she had a feeling that her name had probably gone wrong for ever now. The man took no notice of her actual words.

"Good," he said. "Understand you found ring belonging Mrs Willis, Osmington, you properly public spirited, honest, and Willis came offer reward, so?"

"Yes," said Alice, when she had worked out what the words left out the speech had to be.

"Congratulate," said the man. "Gazette small article picture, permitted?"

"It's neither nowt nor summat," said Dad. "You'll be hard up for news if that's famous."

"Generous refuse reward offer charity," said the man. "Mrs Willis impressed call office."

"You hear all sorts of tales," said Dad.

"Interesting choose favourite charity," said the man. "Why choose?"

"You've got to like something best," said Alice. "But it wasn't like that at all."

"Smile, stand next mother, nice," said the man, and cracked great lights in her face so that his face turned black when Alice looked at it. "Friday. Going Bishop next part story. How old, Alison? Hobby? Brothersister?"

"Twelve," said Alice, which was not true yet, and "riding", which wasn't either, and "no brothersister", which was a lie, not merely untrue.

"Thank," said the man, and went.

"If you tell anyone I'm in the paper," said Alice, "I'll."

"You'll what?" said Mum. "You'll like it when you see it, and other people will see for themselves."

"Staring at me," said Alice.

"Tabby can look at the queen," said Dad.

12

NOBODY LOOKED AT Alice on Friday, or if they did she did not happen to be looking that way. Alice fingered through the local paper at the shop on her way to school, and saw her picture and left it at that, with LOCAL SCHOOLGIRL'S CHARITABLE OFFER written underneath it. Your own photograph is the person with its image facing away from you, unknown, but Alice had gone by Mum, surprised to see how she was shrinking. She glimpsed the Gazette's version of her name, Alison Dyerson, and went to school. She had missed Raddy this morning, so she went round the proper way. At school no one said anything.

Mum was different. "Look," she said, waiting at the office window when Alice came home, and calling her across among the papers and preservatives and pamphlets and the hanging cigarette smoke of customers, "I don't mind if you let the man get your name wrong; I don't mind that your photograph looks as half-witted . . ."

"Gaumless," said Dad, in the next room.

". . . as an empty sock with a hole in it; I don't mind about your imaginary hobby . . ."

"I was just thinking hobby-horse," said Alice.

". . . I don't mind Matthew getting put out of existence . . ."

"I can't remember everything," said Alice.

". . . but I do mind when you haven't told me the rest of the story; I do think it's the sort of thing you should have asked somebody about."

"I don't know what you're cross about," said Alice. "I truly don't. If it was me I'd send you to bed until you'd got over it."

"It's them Willises," said Dad, from the doorway. "I tell you, they've got more motor than sense."

"Not according to the paper," said Mum. "I know they've got a lot wrong, but it can't all be without foundation."

"There's nowt moithering you but that other folk telled you of it first," said Dad, getting away with two local words and one bit of local grammar without being corrected.

"That's only part," said Mum. "Come on, Alice, just tell me, so that I know."

"I tell you what," said Alice, "I'll go to bed and I'll get up when *you* feel better, because I don't know what you are talking about."

"Charitable offer is what it's about," said Mum. "Yes, I can tell you know what I mean: I can read you like a . . . newspaper."

"Yes," said Alice. "I saw the headline thing, but I didn't think about it meaning anything, and I saw your picture . . ."

"And that means less and less too," said Mum.

". . . so I knew it was mine next to you, and I saw the names were wrong, and that's all."

"Read the rest," said Mum.

"Local schoolgirl, Alison Dyerson, 12, does good by stealth," Alice read. "I didn't steal anything."

"It means secretly," said Mum. Alice read on. She had, she learned, found a valuable ring and taken it to the police, and that was right so far. Then the owner, Mrs Willis, had come round with the reward, and this girl Alison had refused it and asked for it to be given to her favourite charity, "a quite unexpected choice, Mrs Willis said, but her own. I thought she meant the animal shelter or an earthquake fund, but she chose it should go to a community of Anglican nuns."

"I knew about the nuns," said Alice. "But that was accident, they didn't understand when I said none of the charities was a favourite. But I told you they came to give something away for me. They never asked me; they just did it. Have I got to read on about the bishop?"

"No need," said Mum. "This Mrs Willis asked him to choose a community of sisters to have the money."

"How much money?" said Alice. "Look, fifty pounds. Well, it's a good thing I didn't know about it or I'd have kept it. Fifty pounds."

"Money well spent for them Willises," said Dad. "It'd cost more than that to get an advertisement that long, and you can't buy bishops for things like that. I mean, he's just in trade, like me, is Willis, only not so common-like."

"Well, we've got that settled," said Mum. "But what's your Grandpa going to say? I've been dreading him ringing up all day, and I'd 've felt so foolish not knowing."

Grandpa telephoned later in the evening. He sent a message through Mum that he was very impressed with what Alice had done and he hoped it was from the right motives, but that did not mean he had anything to say about the Willises.

He was to come to lunch on Sunday, after coming to the morning service at the Minster. He wanted Alice to come up a little early to that service and speak to the bishop. But she was not to become proud.

"No fancying yourself," said Dad. But Mum had not mended her mood by the end of the day, and wasn't going to have priestly advice about Alice's soul confused with advice on how to conduct yourself socially. However,

Alice and Dad were not quite clear about the difference, and Mum got angrier and angrier until she went off to bed.

"She's tired," said Dad. "We've a lot on for the time of year; we're cutting a lot of trees, and oft times you can't see the wood for the paperwork."

Mum came back in about ten minutes. "It's no good going to bed," she said. "I don't sleep when I get there, and I think that's what's making me short-tempered."

"And your arithmetic doesn't add up either all the time," said Dad. "But come to think, I'm not sleeping so well either. Nowt wrong wi'me, but there's summat in the house, I keep thinking, and I get up to look three and four times a night, and then lie waking and thinking on't."

"I've been up too," said Mum. "But you seem well asleep when I do. I keep hearing Alice moving about, but she's always asleep."

"The loft was empty," said Dad. "But there's summat. I keep fancying it's fish in the walls, daft thought."

"Or birds flying in them," said Mum.

"Well, that's not likely," said Dad.

"Nor are fish," said Mum. "Birds are less impossible."

"Birds are impossible," said Dad. "There isn't the space. But fish, well, anyone knows that's a fancy, a similar-like, or whatever they call them at school, Alice."

"Conger-eel," said Alice. "I haven't heard anything at all. I just go to sleep."

Then she was sent off to do just that going to sleep. As she undressed she wondered whether she heard a slithering, swimming, flying, in the walls of the house. She thought there was no sound for her ears, but perhaps a sensation in the top of her skull, like an idea moving its fins or feathers, an idea that she was the cause of the noise, that the noise was made in a way by her, or for her, or that she could do something about it. Then once again she had the whole matter sorted out, and fell asleep.

Sunday morning was frosty. There were leaves on the windows like ivy; there were needles of frost on the trees outside, and when Alice filled the kettle before breakfast the cold water coming in turned the handle of it suddenly chill in her fingers, like the nozzle of a petrol pump when it fills a tank.

The frost brought a white and blue day, with the sun rising and licking all the town roofs, Minster, churches, chapels and houses, so that they became wet and bright and clear, drawn with the finest pen. Dad went outside and stamped on the ground. He was pleased to have frost begin, because of difficulties with getting wagons to felled trees. The sun he frowned at and did not need.

Alice went up before Mum and Dad to the Minster. She went as the bells began to clatter across the cold. She knew what she had to expect across the kirkyard; first a strong feeling of not wanting to go that way at all; and then a stronger one of certainly not wanting to go to church, but that was a feeling she was quite used to, and it was not much worse than a feeling of not wanting to go to school or the dentist, and nearly everyone can manage those nearly all the time; and then there was the actual difficulty of getting across the ground, because the slope seemed steeper, the Minster seemed further away, the ground was slippery and the air itself pushed against her. But now she knew there was peace inside the building, and that helped.

Ice fell on her from the kirkyard trees; the frosted grass on the ground twisted its points towards her and the rime on the blades was pulled off by the wind and rose into her face as water and small shot of ice. Round her there was a local gather of fog and storm, pushing her back, away from where she was going.

It was difficult to breathe. Ice, like sand, flew into her nostrils, and, when she opened her mouth, lodged in the back of her throat so that she thought she must suffocate or at least spit on the path, because of the clinging chemical taste of the fog. She did not know whether she was crying or merely having tears whipped from her eyes.

Go back, said her choking throat, but she made herself take another step and another. Round her there came a thicker and thicker fog and a darkness, and the clash of the Minster bells receded and approached as if she were no longer in the kirkyard.

Something touched her back, something heavy. No, nothing heavy, but something she was leaning on. Light had come round her again. The Minster bells had separated and sweetened; the fog and whirl of ice had gone. She was back in now again, or in something like it. Perhaps it was then she had got to, because in front of her stood a man very little taller than herself, looking at her.

Now we do go home, said her throat, because her general opinion was that something had gone wrong with the world and it was now seven years from now or a hundred years ago, but might be more normal somewhere else, out of the kirkyard.

"My grand-daughter," said Grandpa, who was the heavy thing behind her, on whom she leaned, or who perhaps was pushing. "Dreaming, I am afraid."

No, real, said her throat. The rest of her had no time to say anything about it, because Grandpa went on talking, and Alice went on walking with him and the smaller man. Alice was not listening very well because she had seen on the hand of the smaller man something that she wanted. On one of the fingers of his right hand there was a ring with a red stone. It seemed to her that all she had to do was put out her hand and take it, and that was what she

was meant to do. She put out her hand, and had her finger
and thumb on the ring. But then reality became more real,
as if she had in fact been dreaming and her throat had been
wrong. She found she was doing something so ordinary
and commonplace that she must be in the here and now
of life. She was shaking hands with the bishop, and her
throat was saying how do you do, but the words were
not really coming from her mouth. Then the ring was
out of her reach and she was blushing, sure that she had
been ridiculous and impolite, and angry as well that
something had thrust another ring at her for its unknown
reasons.

But the storm had gone. She walked with Grandpa and
the bishop to the door of the Minster in the calm of a clear
frosty day, and that was all. At the Minster she opened the
door for them, and went in after them. The bishop talked a
little about the charitable gift. Mum and Dad had thought
she did not know what she was doing, just through being
a child; the bishop thought she had been chosen to direct
the gift towards God's purpose, which implied that she
had some special fitness in His eyes but then, the bishop
went on, we all have. Then he smiled at both of them and
walked away alone.

"He lifts you up and puts you down," said Grandpa.

"Oh Grandpa," said Alice, "it wasn't me at all. They just
did it themselves."

"Don't be too humble," said Grandpa. "That's a kind
of pride too." Then he had to go as well. Alice waited in
the transept for Mum and Dad.

While she was in this peaceful building she began to
wonder why it had become so for her. She thought for a
moment or two about holiness coming on, and decided
it wasn't that; holiness was not going to suit the colour of
her eyes, as if it were a dress that was of the wrong pattern.

As well as that, she was not quite sure about God, because of the difficult rule that if you couldn't prove he was there then that proved he was, and she knew that was an unfair rule, but if you said so then people said that God had made it, and that was no help.

She had more proof of something else. She was more and more sure that something had come from the Eyell and that it was going round with her, that it was in the house, and everywhere but in the Minster. And that was sad for it, whatever it was, because it was not a wicked thing. She knew she would know a wicked thing when it came near. She was just deciding that if she could tell what was wicked then she could tell what was God, when Mum and Dad came, and she went for the books for them.

Then the organ music started, and under it she could not tell whether knowing what was wicked proved there was God, any more than full proved the existence of empty.

After the service, and outside once more, she felt herself found again and followed, as if her own dog had looked round and noticed she was there, waiting for her to know its name. And tie it to herself with a ring. But she did not need to be told that; there are things you know without being told: even cats know that your eyes are what you see them with; it was that sort of knowing that made Alice sure captivity was in a ring.

Next Thursday Alice found another ring. It was Market Day, and the traders in the square were moving away. Alice walked across the cobbles through the drifts of tissue paper and straw and newspaper, and there it was, a glittering circle of gold on a cobble. Alice thought of what she suspected about rings and the follower and walked past it.

She stopped. She turned, and looked again. It was a plain gold ring, no jewels, no patterns, lying smooth and foreign on the dark stone. Near it lay a small and rotting potato and a screwed up lettuce leaf.

Alice picked up the ring, carefully between finger and thumb of her left hand. Nothing happened. It was a ring she had found, not a ring that had found her. It would only find her when she placed it on her finger, and she knew she was not going to do that.

All the same, said her throat, I think it wants to marry me. But she knew her throat was wrong. It was more to do with taking a gift, though it was not quite that either. She did not know, she did not know.

She took the finger and thumb of her right hand and let them almost meet in the circle of the ring. What happened then was quite clear, and not alarming, and not sudden. The closer her right hand finger and thumb were together the clearer grew her understanding of what was watching her, what had come from the Eyell. She was not startled. It was nothing evil, nothing splendid, nothing good, nothing foul. It was there, and for that time it was enough to know. She pulled her right hand away, bent down and pulled from some rubbish the wind was moving past her a square of blue tissue paper that had wrapped an apple. She wrapped the ring in it in place of the apple, put the flat packet in her sleeve, walked across to the police station, opened the door, went in, put the packet on the counter.

"That was an original idea," said the policeman she and Raddy had seen last time, pleased to see her.

"Other people are always having them," said Alice. "Here's another," and walked out.

"Wait a minute," said the policeman, but his words did not count, Alice thought; she was at the door and away. Still free.

Not long after tea there was a knock at the door. "I'll go," said Alice. "It won't be for me."

"I don't see the sense in that remark," said Mum. She had been catching everybody up all the evening, and Dad dared not speak at all now.

At the door there was Yvonne, Miss Bennet. "Alison?" she said.

"Alice," said Alice. "Come in."

"I'd like to see your mother," said Yvonne, or perhaps it was the Miss Bennet side of her; Alice wasn't sure.

"I'll get her," she said.

"Don't go right away," said Miss Bennet, not Yvonne, "I want to see you as well."

They went into the dining room. It was about the afternoon's ring. Miss Bennet wanted to know very much more about it than Alice knew. Miss Bennet had the ring with her this time, with the police label on it. Mum knew nothing about it at all, because Alice had said nothing: the ring problem was something between Alice and the thing she had begun to think of now as IT. IT was bringing her rings, and she was getting rid of them. But there was no way she could begin to explain that to anyone else, and all she had was the simple story of the truth about the afternoon.

Miss Bennet made her tell it twice, and made notes in her book about it. Then she sat and looked at Alice without saying anything for a while. She turned to Mum. "You haven't lost a ring like this, have you, Mrs Dyson?"

"Here's my ring," said Mum, rapping her hand flat on the table. "You've heard Alice through twice, and that's her story and she's told it." Mum was properly angry now, and her hand on the table shook so that the ring rattled on the wood. Alice grew angry too. She had done two right things with the ring, by not wearing it and by handing it in, and there was no third thing that was right too, if the truth would not do.

"We felt we had to make enquiries," said Miss Bennet. "It's very odd for it to happen twice. Some young girls might want to draw attention to themselves when it has . . ."

She stopped speaking. Mum had taken her hand away from the table and now no one was touching it. The table went on shaking a little and the ring Miss Bennet had brought, standing on its own glow and reflection, was dancing a little on the wood, like a coin at the end of its spinning. Only this busy vibration was not at the end of a spinning but by itself.

Alice looked and saw and felt her anger stretch out. For her, for a moment, the ring stood still again, and the room moved, not the ring; and in that moment's standing, with no one close to it, it flew from the table and lobbed up on the Welsh dresser and rattled behind the blue plate on a high shelf.

The room stood still again. But everything in it moved: the curtains belled out, the three chairs in the corners moved inwards, the dresser itself slid away from the wall, the sideboard scraped its feet on the parquet, the chairs they sat on pulled them closer to the table, and the table itself rose a little way into the air, tipped, and stayed so. Underfoot the carpet hunched and rippled, as if they stood on a huge dog; it was the carpet that had raised the table and moved the chairs in.

"What's this?" said Dad, coming in, and seeing first the lamp fitting swaying overhead. "What the devil . . ."

"Oh," said Miss Bennet, "has it stopped? I think I . . ."

"She has, by God," said Dad, because Miss Bennet had stood up, taken one step away from the table, and begun to fall over. Dad caught her. "Now what?" he said.

"We'll go in the other room," said Mum, firmly. Dad watched her, holding Miss Bennet, and puzzled when Mum went to the dresser and pulled the ring from the upper shelf. "Why that didn't all fall down I don't know," she said. "Alice."

Alice followed into the other room. Mum closed the dining room behind them.

Alice remembered after that Miss Bennet, much more Yvonne-like, sipping at a glass, and Dad going out with her and starting the car. Alice herself was aware of being tired, and then knew from moment to moment that she was being put into bed by Mum, and that was all until quite broad daylight the next day, with the house quiet, and the Minster clock sounding a half hour, and then a three-quarters, and then as many strokes as possible for mid-day. Alice got herself up, ate three bowls of cornflakes, and went back to bed again and did last night's homework, comfortable and quiet, until Mum came at one o'clock and looked at her.

"I don't know why you used three separate bowls and three spoons," she said.

"Three helpings," said Alice.

"You wouldn't wake this morning," said Mum. "I left you. But you might as well get up; I don't think there's anything wrong with you, and you can get along to school. Can you eat any more?"

"Yuk," said Alice.

She went to school for the afternoon. Mum sent a note saying she had been at home for observation, which sounded quite official, though Alice hadn't observed anything.

On the way out she saw the dining room door standing open. All was perfectly tidy inside, but rather cleaner than it should be on a Friday when dusting day was Saturday. Then she took her stomachful of milk slopping to school.

13

"YOU DIDN'T GO last year," said Mum. "You had chicken-pox."

"Did I?" said Alice.

"Your best Christmas present was a bottle of calamine lotion," said Mum. "But you went the year before."

"Probably where I caught chickenpox," said Alice. "But I don't want to go to St Hilda's party with Arethusa Willis."

"Andrea, isn't it?" said Mum.

"She called me Alison," said Alice. "A on the envelope and Alison inside. Can I have a bad squint this year instead?"

"You've got two more letters to open," said Mum. "Better have a look at them first."

So it was fixed that she went to the party. The next letter was from one of the Governors of the Minster Schools, Grandpa, who invited her to the same party; and the third was from Matthew, because the other Minster School was the Choir School, and that invited her as well.

"I thought as much," said Mum.

"You knew as much,' said Alice.

"Of course I did," said Mum. "And you're going, and if you've got a bad squint you can close one eye, and if you've got chickenpox you can take your bottle of lotion, and that settles you. So stay where you are, and I'll clear the breakfast, and you write back at once."

Alice wrote three answers. One was to Matthew, saying that Miss Dyson gratefully accepted the kind invitation; the next was to Grandpa, a proper letter, saying that she had already accepted Matthew's invitation, if he wanted to invite someone else instead; and the third to Miss A. Willis, saying the same thing.

"You could have telephoned Grandpa," she said.

"It all has to be done properly for him," said Mum. "Anyone else, yes, but not him. You know that."

"I'll telephone Arethusa," said Alice. But she had to put pen to paper. Mum stood by, being very gentle and kind, because they had both discovered that if Alice lost her temper then things began to fly about the room. It was something Mum had worried about a lot at first, but now she and Alice had become used to the trouble. Mum now only worried about it when it happened, not when it wasn't happening, but took care to see that Alice stayed in a good mood. Alice herself knew when she was going into a rage and had to close her eyes and think herself out of the bad mood. There were other times when things happened, and the chief one she noticed was when Raddy had an effect on her, and she on Raddy. It had been at its worst when Dad had been locked in the roof, and since then it had banged shop doors all along Kirk Alley, knocked down some trestles at a market stall, while the stall was being put up, and Alice was sure it had caused one car to run into the back of another, leaving a lot of broken red plastic in the road from the lamps.

Raddy said she knew what it was, after several such events, and now she sometimes chose to walk to school with Edward and Nell and the others, which didn't mean that she was getting away from Alice, but she explained that strange things happened when she had been to church earlier, and they didn't happen on other days, or when she was with the others and Alice walked with them all. Alice was glad to walk with them all, so it worked out well.

The letter-writing caused no upset. Alice was not sure whether it just hadn't, or whether she had kept her temper. Temper is not a thing you can be sure about or see far ahead: on it comes, and you have to be ready.

"It'll go away," said Mum.

"Yours didn't," said Alice.

"Not the temper, the extra bit," said Mum. Alice concluded that there was temper, and nasty temper, and nasty temper was what she had, like chickenpox but without the useful bottle of lotion. She wondered about the lotion, though. The other thing that must belong to the same set was the difficulty in getting to the Minster. She had found a way of dealing with that, though it involved a sort of lie. She would say to herself that she was just going to the shops, or to catch a bus, and then she would be allowed quite close to the Minster door, and could make a dash for it, and find peace inside.

What she had got, she thought, was something naughty, playing certain tricks on her and other people, and being quite a nuisance about one thing, the bringing of rings.

There were three more rings, after the plain one in the Market Place. The first was almost certainly a curtain ring, and she kicked that into a road drain and it splashed down into the sump. The next had been all three parts of one of those rings that is made of three interlocking bands of an odd shape; she had found all three parts separated and lying on the kirkyard wall. With a twig she had pushed them into a heap and put them in a damp tissue from her pocket, taking the tissue to the river, and dropped it in when no one was looking, because it was, after all, leaving litter about in a public place. The tissue had sailed away, the good ship Kleenex.

The third had come rolling along Eye Street one day when she had gone to the shop. She had almost disregarded it, because it was too small for a finger, and was probably part of an ear-ring. She had picked it up and taken it away, however, in case some child found it, since it was obviously being presented to her along with the other rings.

The party was the next tiresome thing. "Don't get into a fuss," said Mum. "You know."

"I can feel I'm making faces with my neck," said Alice. "You know."

"Not with the back of," said Mum. "Bend over again." She was washing Alice's hair at the edge of the bath. Alice could feel that all-over coldness that parties bring starting to descend from the top of her head. Soon there was to be cold hair against her neck, with the low collar of a party dress, and then the coolness of the cloth coming through her vest at the tied-in waist, and then the nothingness of new white tights, and the shoeless feeling of party pumps.

"At least my bloomers don't show through my dress," said Alice. "Theirs all will."

"Are you going to take a shawl or a cardigan?" said Mum.

Alice took a shawl. Then it was time to go. Cold air outside crawled along her scalp. "Come out in my nightie, I'm sure," said Alice, and her shivering jaw made her bite her tongue and a sudden jewel of tear stood along each eye and pulled all the horizons into marvellous shapes as they went to St Hilda's.

"I'll be at Grandpa's," said Mum. "He'll be at the party some of the time but I think he likes tea at home. Matthew's coming back for the night, did I tell you."

"I don't want to go in," said Alice. "I've got the squint in both eyes."

"That's normal," said Mum. "Go on; see you later."

Alice trudged up the front steps, carrying her pumps.

The party was completely enjoyable, except for three things that were not its fault at all. Alice walked the length of the School Governors and staff, shaking hands with Grandpa and with the bishop, the two she knew. The bishop wore his ring still, and it pressed on her hand again, but she was not inclined to put her finger and thumb on it. Then she went to find Matthew, and that was a good thing because they were pleased to see each other, and Alice, particularly, did not want to talk to anyone else, though Matthew had his school friends.

It was a much noisier party than Alice had expected. She had not looked forward to all the minuets and dainty dances and the staircase music, up and down, she thought would be there. But the music seemed right, just like the Canal pub music drifting up the road on a Saturday night.

There were one or two of the older sorts of dance, in which the bishop and other Governors could join, and there were games, and after losing Matthew and regretting that she forgot him.

There was crowded tea in the school dining room, but there was no need to sit down. There were crackers to pull, which led a fat girl to sit on the bishop, who was smaller than she was, and he put his elbow on a small girl's nose. Alice shook her cracker and the trinket inside thudded. She knew what she would get and decided not to pull it with anyone. But one of the boys came up and she had to pull it with him. The ring she expected dropped out among the plates on the table. It was a big one for a cracker, she thought. She told herself it was quite safe to put this one on, because it was not brought to her by IT; but she could see herself thinking as well that if she did put it on she would know what IT wanted. She picked it up.

There was quiet beginning round her. She had listened to her own thoughts and forgotten the party. Now the headmistress of St Hilda's was calling for a moment's silence and was talking, but Alice was hardly hearing. "If anyone has found it please bring it to me," said the headmistress, but Alice did not know what. She twisted the ring round and was about to put it on.

"No reward this time," said the bishop, holding out his hand, with the pale mark on his finger where his ring had been.

"Oh, thank you," said Alice, understanding what she had not quite heard the headmistress say, that the bishop had mislaid his ring. She put the ring in the bishop's palm. "It's only from a cracker," she said.

"I have sometimes wondered about that myself," said the bishop. He slipped it on to his finger. "Your token must have gone astray," he said.

"Do you understand things better when you have that ring on?" said Alice.

"I am supposed to," said the bishop. "But it is not always so. Why do you ask? We have met before, have we not? You are the girl that found another ring some time ago, about which there was a silly fuss concerning the reward? I thought so. Again, why do you ask your question?"

"This is the seventh or ninth ring I have found," said Alice. "I nearly put this one on to see what they were for."

"I see," said the bishop. "Come to my house, which is called the palace, for tea on Boxing Day."

"I'll ask Mum," said Alice.

"And now we must find that token," said the bishop.

"No," said Alice, "it'll only be another ring."

The party went on. The bishop left, and Grandpa had gone

before tea. Alice had a few words with Andrea, but they were mostly Andrea's words about a super pony called Nijinsky.

The headmistress came up to her a little later and pulled her from a game called Indigestion, which they had invented at St Hilda's.

"I'd like to talk to you," she said. "Let's go into my room where it's quiet."

I'll give it to the nuns again, said Alice's throat, since Alice herself thought it must be a reward coming along after all.

"Sit down by the fire," said the headmistress. She was a tall person with a very wide neck, and had played hockey for England and once went in for a town-crier's competition and won it, and there was the certificate to say so on the wall in a frame.

"Yes, it's quite true," said the headmistress, seeing Alice read it. "It's the one essential qualification for running St Hilda's."

Apart from green knickers, thought Alice.

"I have a very odd little piece of paper here," said the headmistress. "Do you recognize it?"

Alice knew it. It was her entrance examination paper. It had her name on it, and then her name, and then her name a number of times more, and that was all.

"We thought it was very original," said the headmistress. "That's a word with a good meaning; it means you are a person with your own thoughts and opinions. So we were quite glad to see that, and sorry that the very good idea you had made it impossible for us to offer you a place at the school last year. We know you are original, and we know you are intelligent too."

If I'd been really intelligent, thought Alice, I'd have put someone else's name.

"We'd like to know why you don't want to come here. Because that's what it is, isn't it? You can come here without having to pay, you know, and you don't have to be a boarder, if either of those things bothered you. Don't say anything now, Alice, but think about it. Early next year there is another entry examination, and since you will then be twelve you could gain a scholarship, which is the way of not having to pay fees. We'd like you to try the exam again, and then, when you've truly thought about it, decide whether you want to join us. There now, that's all; you can run along now. Oh dear, I shouldn't have said that; it's what I would say to one of our own girls. I really mean, let's go back and join the party."

Alice went downstairs again upset and cross. She had known from the moment of getting the invitations that she had not wanted to come to this party; now she was at it they were spoiling it by reminding her of a time when she had managed things badly, and making her feel foolish. She went back into the gymnasium where the party was going on, and stood inside the door. She could feel herself getting crosser and she knew she was going to be angry soon, but there was nothing near that she knew to fasten herself to with a look or a hold or familiarity. Then she began to hold her rage, to resist the temptation to be nasty.

"I feel sick," said a voice beside her. It was Matthew, and he looked pale and his mouth drooped and he had his hand at his throat.

"It's their rotten food," said Alice. "I hate them all," and the paperchains and streamers and pendants the gym was hung with began to sway, and the ventilating windows fell open, a whirl of wind fetched everybody to a standstill, and black things flew about the room: the records had lifted from their place by the player and were flying. The music stopped.

"Where's the toilet?" said Matthew.

"Oh, shut up," said Alice, pushing him out of the room. "Go and get your coat."

A few seconds later, before Matthew had time to feel any worse, which he did soon, they were going down the steps and across the gravel and along the drive to the road.

At the gates Matthew had to stop and lean on the wall and put his head through the ornamental railings. Then he came and walked beside her crying and smelling rather vile.

So they walked along in the dark, Matthew snuffling, and Alice getting the better of her temper and thinking how hopeless it was to be herself when there was nothing left to do but the dullest things of life. Even the headmistress had blocked off a tiny corner by being winner of the town-crier's competition.

At first they walked in the dark, and then they came to the first street lamp of Sarrow. Then, somewhere between the second lamp and the third, was Sarrow Cross, quite plain to see. Matthew had stopped his sobs now, and was looking about a bit.

"Beadlam Cross," he said. He was getting like Grandpa, telling all he knew all the time. "It looked like a person at first." Then he had to stop and spit out some fragments still in his mouth. Alice thought of other things and tried not to know what his mouth must be like inside.

It was not difficult to think of other things. They were there, waiting to be thought of, but only by Alice. Matthew did not see them.

By the Cross people were standing, or almost standing. There was something shadowyer than the shadows they were in, something incomplete about them, as they stood, and moved a little.

Alice was not alarmed, only a little startled. She knew, in some way, that she had not seen them with her eyes but in some other way, and that they were only part of all the other things that had become apparent to her. And as well as that she was so tired that she was not clear about anything.

She walked on. Matthew followed. They came to Sarrow Vicarage. Alice went straight to the car and got in and went to sleep. Matthew walked on alone to the house.

14

"BANKRUPT," SAID THE BISHOP. "You have taken all my property, all my money, and now I can't pay you ten pounds for winning the beauty competition."

"Oh," said Alice. "But I haven't finished playing yet. You can go on if you like, because I want to build two hotels on Mayfair."

"You've won everything," said the bishop. "Now we'd better put it all away and send you home. Did you know you cheated all through the game?"

"You can't cheat to Monopoly," said Alice. "I was lucky with the dice."

"That's what I mean," said the bishop. "They did exactly what you wanted, didn't they?"

"But you're allowed to want them to do anything you like," said Alice. "I was lucky."

"No," said the bishop, "not lucky. You knew what you were doing, didn't you?"

"You mean, if I wanted a seven I could throw one?" said Alice.

"Exactly that," said the bishop. "It is true, isn't it?"

"It can't be true," said Alice. "I mean it can have happened, but I can't have had anything to do with it because you can't have anything to do with things like that. And I wasn't throwing all your bad throws, was I?"

"You were changing the numbers on all the throws, when you remembered," said the bishop. Alice shook her head. The bishop seemed to change the subject. "What was happening to you in the churchyard the first time we met?" he asked.

"One of those terrible Minster winds," said Alice, gathering up all the green twenty notes.

"It was your own private snowstorm," said the bishop. "I saw it for myself. It vanished when I came up to you, I remember."

It's the way you throw the dice, said Alice's throat.

"And tell me about the rings," said the bishop. "How many?" and he stacked the fifty pound notes on the twenties. Alice had once counted the fifties, and all the other Monopoly notes, and known how many of those there were; but it was not of those that the bishop was speaking and a funny answer would not do.

"Seven or nine," said Alice, "depending on whether you count the love-knot one as one or three."

"Then tell me," said the bishop, "two things: what is responsible for private snowstorms and wandering rings, because you remember that mine wandered from my finger, and therefore for cheating at Monopoly; and what would happen if you put on one of the rings."

"O.K.," said Alice. "If I put one of the rings on I'd be in charge, but I don't know the other bit, what I'd be in charge of. There's something. I call it IT."

"Where is IT?" said the bishop. "Near the Minster? Near you?"

"Near me," said Alice. "I don't know whether IT came from the Minster or the Eyell. I was digging and it followed me home afterwards, and it's usually all right until I lose my temper or get too near the Minster, and sometimes it's a bit funny with my friend Raddy."

Alice sorted out a great pile of one pound notes and put them in the box. The bishop put in the Community Chest cards.

"It'll be some sort of spirit," he said calmly, as if he were saying some bird was a starling. "The Minster started as a missionary church, you know, and it would be built in some important place, where worship was already carried out, because people like continuity. God isn't the only spirit, you see; he happens to be the only God among them, and that's what makes the difference. But you've got a problem with yours, haven't you?"

"I have?" said Alice.

"It makes you cheat at Monopoly," said the bishop. "Or you let it help you."

"You're supposed to win," said Alice. "There's nothing about it in the rules."

Then the bishop laughed and said she was mistaken, and pulled a huge bible from a shelf and showed her a list of rules she already knew of, called the Ten Commandments, and said there should be a copy of it in every set of Monopoly, though no one would play the game any more. Then he sent Alice home, after she had promised to remember the rules existed even if she did not know exactly what they said.

One morning towards the end of January Alice woke up cold and deaf. When she looked from her window she saw only red and white light until she scraped away frost inside. Then there was clear sky above, a rim of red morning cloud, and all the wood stacks had grown tall in the night where snow had fallen silently and lined itself up with the wood with the same cut ends and bark-like edges. The silence beyond, in the town, was torn away by a clanging scrape from a snow-plough drawing its blade along the road.

Dad was already up. This was the weather that pleased

him, when he could haul wood. Mum got up and went out to the office to turn on the heater. Alice got up too, though it was Saturday. She had thought of throwing snow at someone without being certain who was to get it.

"Right Christmas weather," said Dad, "if it was the time of year. I'll walk up to Sarrow and we'll get out that oak tree I've been waiting for. It makes you want to be outside, does a day like this."

"There's room for all sorts of opinions," said Mum. "I can tell you."

Alice put on two pairs of socks and her rubber boots before breakfast, and in the middle of the meal remembered the knitted cap with earpieces, and put that on as well, until Mum told her to take it off or she would not feel the benefit when she got outside.

"Are you coming up with me?" said Dad. "There's nowt to see; we're nobbut dragging a tree off a bank. Come up for the company and then walk back."

"Take a basket with you," said Mum. "I'll make a list."

"Yes, yes," said Alice, without any intention of going to Sarrow with Dad or of going shopping for Mum. She wanted to live the day on snow with no thought of anything else and with no one else.

But she had the basket and the list and Dad, and there was really nothing wrong with those things, which stopped her standing about and getting cold.

They went out across the kirkyard, but not near the Minster itself, and then up through the streets where the plough had heaped the road snow on the pavements and it was all sugar-mountaineering, crisp underfoot if you walked in the fresh parts, but slippery where anyone had trodden first. The frost still held, and their breath hung round them in clouds.

They came out of the clogged streets and walked over the

fields to the top of Sarrow Hill, and there Alice looked back and saw the town had become entirely roofless against the distant white hills. She had seen the Minster like it before, but not every tile of the other building covered. The place was no longer there; or the drawing was not yet complete.

"Going in to see Grandpa?" said Dad. "You could, you know."

But Alice felt she could not: he would not be pleased to see her. All she did was use the bushes inside his front gate as a hiding place for the basket, and then walked on with Dad to where the tree was to be dragged away.

"Away, you lads," he said to no one, because the lads he was wanting had not yet arrived.

"They're yonder," said Alice. "Oh no, it's the Cross."

"We'll hear them first," said Dad. "They've got the wagon."

"I'm just going to look at the Cross," said Alice. "Don't go out of sight." It was not the treecutters she had seen, but something much more shadowy, people she had seen before, round the Cross. She said to herself that she should be frightened, and should have been frightened before, but she was only curious, and a little pitying, but she did not know she should be that. But unfrightened or not, she would not have approached even in this brightest of days unless Dad had been there.

She came closer to the Cross. There were no marks on the ground near it, but there were moving people there. It was hard to see them. They had been indistinct in the dark and they were the same now, and when she come nearer they were possibly less visible, or perhaps only less clear, than they had been from further away. There was nothing to be alarmed about. The people did not see her, though as she came nearer they seemed to become busier, but what they were busy at she could not tell.

She went to the Cross and touched it, then turned and walked back to Dad. "I'll go home," she said.

"Aye, do that," said Dad. "You'll starve here wi' me."

Alice walked off, but not the way she had just come, by the Cross, or down the fields the way she and Dad had arrived here. She went along the road, to get herself into the proper part of town for the shopping.

Lazy Cross was on her road. This was the Cross to the west of the town, near the bishop's palace. By it there was a queue of people waiting for a bus, and she did not like to look too hard at them to see how distinct they were. She thought they looked convincingly real, not shadowy in the least. She could not even look for shadowy people without staring at the others.

She went on. By the market she met Raddy.

"Didn't know you," said Raddy. "Ho'd on while I get a baw of snow, little Fred riding hood with your basket."

"Town snow is mucky," said Alice. "Let's get in the kirkyard later when I've done the shopping."

"When I see you," said Raddy. "I've shopping and all," and then they found they were going different ways, and parted. A piece of hard snow struck Alice on the shoulder, and she saw Raddy grinning at her. Alice cheated then, and knew she had. She did not throw any snow, but when she looked at a windowsill full of it above Raddy's head she knew it was herself that made it tip on Raddy's head. Though of course it could not be. But she knew it was.

Raddy shrugged her shoulders, laughed, and walked on, not quite sure what had happened. Thou shalt not, thought Alice, snowdrift thy neighbour.

She took the shopping home by a very long route because she wanted to think. She went out of the town again and walked along beside the river, where no one had been that day, and where the water was bright as it flowed, and sometimes dark with ice, and in other places had snow shrouding it. She went along the bank, and she felt she had more to carry than the basket of shopping, and more to think of than her own mind could know. She came alone, or not quite alone, because she knew IT was with her, a weightless heaviness. At the bridge she had to leave the waterside and cross the road. She joined the river path at the other side until she came to where the carts went down a notch in the bank when people wanted sand or gravel.

And here she saw more of the shadowy people, standing among the bare barbed strands of bramble and threadless nettle, standing and moving, there and not here, more than smoke, less than shade.

She was not frightened, even though Dad was not there to run to if she felt alarm. She felt that she now knew something about this place, and that the knowledge should be perfectly clear to her, and it was like that moment of brilliance before going to sleep. This one slipped away under the waking sun, however, and she put the thought aside to think of later, and turned away from the people.

She had to turn away because the path went no further. Beyond this point there was a thicket of thorns and then trees fenced off with wire. She had to go back the way she had come or follow a little way up the cart track. The cart track led to the road, but there was another field path beyond, with a clear sign on it, and she took that. She came out among the houses of a council estate, and then into older parts of the town, and all at once was by Easter Cross.

She had been walking, but had become cold. She felt a shiver strike at her, and wondered why. There was a wind beginning to blow, not on her alone, because other people felt it too. What it did for her, besides making her hand holding the basket very cold indeed, was make her eyes water and her nose run. She could not, for the moment, see whether Easter Cross had people near it.

She set her basket down, pulled off her right glove, and found her handkerchief and blew her nose. She was sure she was now like Andrea Willis, with a drop at the end of it. But there was no sneeze.

Then, pulling on her glove, she noticed the final ring. She did not see it on her hand, but only through the glove, the bulge of it. She knew it was not there, that she had not put it on, but it was there, raising the outline of her finger. She felt with the other gloved hand, clumsily, and it was there. She pulled off her right glove. There was nothing on her finger.

She felt the glove, to remove whatever had misled her. The glove was empty of fingers, of rings, of anything.

Then she felt with her bare left hand, and on the third finger of the right hand she felt, though she could not see, a ring. At once she tried to pull it off, but it was like pulling herself away, or as if she pulled nothing. And something else became clear.

The ring was not complete. Three parts of it were there, the top, or the part on the back of the finger; the part on the little finger side; and the part on the palm side; but not the other quarter, the quarter that her thumb would naturally touch when pulling the ring off; the thing she could not do.

She stood there in horror for some time, horror and cold, and the wind licked all the heat from her fingers, until she could not feel anything on any of them. Then she looked up, sure now that she was visited with all the ghosts of the world, and saw at Easter Cross only the same little shadows and frail showings as she had seen at Beadlam Cross.

And, she knew, and at Venwath Cross, because she now knew where that was, not at the road bridge, not at the crossing of the river, but by the ford, the wath, where the carts used to go across by the cut in the bank. When she realized that she realized that she had seen all four Crosses, but only walked round three parts of the circle they made, and that was why she had only three parts of a ring upon her finger.

At that she vowed never to complete the circle, and walked home, no longer cold, and no longer feeling, either, that she was dragging IT with her. IT, for the moment, was out of the way; although she had hardly felt the weight she knew the lightness of its going.

15

THERE WAS NO thaw for several weeks. The fallen snow lay still in still air, grew dirtier underfoot and on roofs, and thinned where the sun shone on it and stayed high where the sun could not shine.

"It's so peaceful," said Mum one day. "Isn't it?"

"The weather?" said Alice.

"And you, I think," said Mum. "Has it all cleared up, whatever it was?"

Alice looked at her hands, which were busy in a tea towel drying some plates. There was still a ring on that finger of the right hand, or three parts of a ring, and she could at times feel it with the other hand, and at other times feel it against her bone, and it showed under her gloves. So IT had not gone entirely away. "I think it's on holiday," she said. "It or IT."

"I'm glad it's not a bother," said Mum.

"You don't seem very bothered, either," said Alice. "It's worse to look back on than be with."

"I'm not terribly worried," said Mum. "I talked to the bishop several times, and we both decided not to worry."

"I played Monopoly," said Alice. "He said I cheated and told me to obey the Ten Commandments."

"And did you?" said Mum.

"Easily," said Alice. "I won't know why Moses had such trouble."

"And Grandpa thought," Mum began, "that . . ."

"Grandpa," said Alice. "Why him?"

"Now, don't get cross," said Mum. "Just go on drying those plates and keep them in one piece."

"Hmn," said Alice, and her throat rattled, quite unable to think of anything to say.

"He thought the trouble would correct itself. Don't forget that I was with him in New Guinea when he was a missionary. I was your age at the time, and I was older, and we are both quite familiar with wandering spirits that attach themselves to people for a time, so at least we knew what was going on. Believe me, we met far worse ones than yours. But of course out there it was much easier to talk about things like that."

But Alice thought she did not want to talk about it any more, because it was her own concern rather than anyone else's.

"I'll write its biography when it's gone," she said. "Just now it hasn't quite." And that was what she knew. There had been peace for some time, but not for all of it entirely. There had been a day when she had met Raddy coming down from the Market with fresh spring flowers for Raddy's church, and walked down with her and merely into the porch, because they wanted to finish a conversation they were having. Alice had not intended to go in, but IT had felt she was going in and had formed into one of its turmoils there and then and ripped the paper from the flowers and then scattered the yellow petals round them and in the church garden. Raddy had begun to cry and Alice had run home very upset, with the frozen snow cracking about her for half the journey, and then everything going back to normal.

One day the sun did not shine through clouds. The afternoon grew warm overhead, but cold was still striking up from the ground. While they were all still at school snow began to fall again. The buses came early for the country children, and school stopped soon after for the rest.

The new snow came down wet and slick, and stuck to the old, turning the town white again, and then became drier, and there was a sharp wind that made it drift and heap and whip at legs and faces. It was on this day that Alice knew something was still seeking for her. She and Raddy had to walk home behind the Market Place because Kirk Alley was blocked by a wagon that had slipped on the slope and wedged against some railings. They had come out the wrong side of the Minster and had to walk a different way through the kirkyard.

"We'll go round," Alice said, because she had seen people among the tombstones. "It's a funeral."

"Nobody there," said Raddy. "Just the stones. And I'd rather go where there was some folk anyroad."

"I'd rather go where there wasn't," said Alice. She thought she had probably seen only shadows again, but it was very hard to be certain about that sort of shadow in falling snow, and she went down through the kirkyard with Raddy, and the wind snapped at their heels, particularly, so that it almost felt as if a dog were there, and they battled, like everyone else, through the storm home like snowmen.

That same wind, by next morning, had dropped all its snow and turned warm and smelt of distant sea. It washed through Alice like water, made her stagger at corners, and kept throwing dirty wet hard pieces of icy snow at her from rooftops and the forks of trees and cracks in walls. It was a Saturday, and in the Market the stallholders of the small market were tying their stalls down and saying how grand it was to see the ground again.

Alice went up the newly hatched pavements to buy nothing, but for the sake of being out and not cold. She went to Raddy's house after doing some phantom shopping. Mrs Larkman said Alison should come in (Sissy put the cat down) since Raddy was still in bed (let pussy alone, Sissy, Cecilia) (Raddy, get yourself out of there) and Alison would think this skip of ironing would never be bottomed and she would be right (Sissy I tell you about that cat there I told you it'll have your nose off no I won't smack pussy) (Raddy will you come on down, my lass) (I'm in a good mind to smack you, not pussy) and would Alison have a cup of tea?

"Let me get in again the fire," said Raddy when she appeared. Alice went to play with Bobby, the littlest Larkman, and wondered whether she had enough authority in the house to wipe his nose, and what with.

"It was too cold to build one before," said Raddy. "And it's not so bad in here by the fire, so shall we?" Mrs Larkman said that was typical, Raddy, and Freddy get your thieving tongue out of the milk, to build a snowman when there was no snow left. Raddy said she would find some and that Alison was going with her.

There was no snow. It was scouring away before their eyes. It was going so fast that the pavements were drying under the wind. There was some snow lying in sheltered places in the kirkyard, but it was like wet salt and miserably cold. Then a fire engine came along quietly and stopped at the other end of the Minster, on the cobbled forecourt there and began to undo its ladders and connect up a hose.

"I could do with a fire," said Raddy, shaking her wet hands. "Leave it, eh?"

"It'll be the Minster," said Alice. "Matthew will have to leave school if it burns down." But before she became very alarmed they could both see that fire was not the trouble.

The firemen were merely washing down the west window because over the winter a coat of ice had formed on it, supported during the frost by the stone arch, but now held only by the glass. The wind was not melting it fast enough, and water gently applied was loosening it and sheets and shards were tumbling down on to the cobbles.

"It isn't very warming," said Raddy. "Is it?"

"We'll go inside," said Alice. "It'll be more mysteriouser from there." And of course as soon as she said that her little local storm started, and the fount of water from the hose wavered, and someone said to hey up and hold on. But the storm was different today. It was not so wild, though it was just as strong. It sent Alice along steadily, and Raddy with her, so that they both thought they would be blown away and crouched small to let the wind blow over them. But at the door on the south side, because they could not get to the one under the west window, the wind stopped, as if they had come into shelter, and Alice felt within her, inside her heart almost, a strong sensation of another's loneliness and despairing sadness and resignation to doing something regrettable; and it all added up to the fact that IT wanted to go into the Minster and asked for her company and protection.

"Come on," she said.

"It's all right," said Raddy. "I can come in if I don't pray."

"It would be best if you didn't," said Alice, because IT was upset by prayer and, she thought, wanted to be away from it, but had to dare go near holy things before being able to escape.

They walked into the Minster, and no strange thing happened except that IT was frightened, and Alice felt a coldness on the fingers of her right hand where the invisible metal hung.

There was noise from the west window, but the glass was too busy and coloured for anything to be seen. They watched and felt warmer, and then wandered away.

"I feel as if I'm going somewhere," said Raddy. "Where?"

"We're looking for something," said Alice.

"Yes," said Raddy. "But this isn't a game, is it? You know, St Antony is quite good at finding things. Shall I ask?"

"No," said Alice.

"I expect it would be prayer," said Raddy. "There aren't any places to pray at, and no candles. It's a dry sort of church, Alice. No pictures even."

They came up the nave and into the choir, where all the carved wood rose from the floor and hung between the pillars, with all round the outside the seats for priests named by their place and position.

"It's beautiful," said Raddy. "But terrible hard seats," and she sat in the back row, under the canopies with spires that went along the walls. "The seat's loose, too, like a toilet seat," and she lifted it up.

The underside of the seat had a small but very complicated carving on it, of ears of wheat and grapes and a man driving an ox.

"Well, look at that," said Raddy. "Did you know?"

"I've never looked," said Alice. "But it's what we came in for, isn't it?"

"Discovery," said Raddy, and lifted the next seat. It had a fox carrying away a goose along the ploughed furrow. The next had swordsmen, and there were strange animals, monstrous fruits, dragons, pelicans, someone who looked like a cyclist but was probably a man on a cart, a tree with a rocket in it ... It was not always easy to tell what the carvings were, and some of them were merely leaves.

"My goodness," said Raddy, at the end of the row, "here's a rude one."

"Go on," said Alice, coming to look from her end of the row, "don't they have Adam and Eve in your church?"

"Not topless," said Raddy, "and bottomless, but that sounds the opposite of what it means."

"I've got one that won't come up," said Alice. "I've got to get it up."

Raddy thought the one she went back to was not meant to come up, because it was boxed in below and all the others could have been seen by lying on your back and looking up.

"Pull at that side," said Alice. "I've got to get in."

"What's in it?" said Raddy.

"Another picture," said Alice. "I've got to see it."

A piece of the Minster came off in their hands. The little seat came away from the wall, the casing below lifted, and there was a cavity made of plain wood at the back and plain floor below.

"Nothing," said Raddy. "And somebody heard that, I know."

"Under the seat," said Alice. And they turned over what they had pulled out.

There was a cross carved below, with a circle round it of small people, and at the middle of the cross was a larger figure.

"What an ugly Jesus," said Raddy.

"It doesn't look like him," said Alice. "It isn't, of course."

"He's on the cross," said Raddy.

"No," said Alice. "The cross is on him, holding him down," and they looked at the ugly imp of a figure that was certainly not Jesus.

"It's got sad eyes," said Raddy.

"Yes," said Alice. "It's depressed, you know," and she

had recognized the figure; she knew she saw the representation of IT.

Mr Tyle came hurrying into the choir. He saw them and came to them, and was so angry he was unable to speak.

"Don't be upset," said Alice, "you don't know what will happen." But Mr Tyle went on being upset, and nothing happened beyond that; IT was not interested in anyone but Alice.

"Give it to me," said Mr Tyle. "Come with me. You'll go to the Dean. This is sacrilege. You'll be sent away. You'll be whipped."

"I'll carry it," said Alice, and she clutched the awkward wooden shape.

"This way," said Mr Tyle. "Look what you've done, look at that hole. You are vandals. It'll be the bishop. You'll be excommunicated. That's pre-Reformation, that is."

He led them to the library.

"I've got to go home," said Raddy.

"It's all right," said Alice. "I've only got to explain, and everything'll be all right."

But when they were in the library she could not begin to explain, because it was not the dean there, or Mr Blackbushe, who would have listened, but Grandpa, and when she saw him she stopped thinking.

"Oh," said Grandpa, taking the wood from her. "Oh. We thought that was all over."

"No," said Alice. "It isn't. But you can't help, Grandpa."

"It's all right, Mr Tyle," said Grandpa. "We have the pieces, and we have the culprit, and I'll see the Dean about it."

"More like a judge and jury," said Mr Tyle. "I'd better go and see what else is happening down there." And he went out, breathing rapidly.

When he had gone Grandpa said, "You'd better go home, Alice, and your friend too. I can help, and I will. Be at home this afternoon."

"I don't get all this," said Raddy. "What's going to happen to us?"

"Nothing," said Grandpa.

"That's no comfort," said Raddy. "Something should."

"There's something else to do," said Alice. "I don't know what it is yet, but there is something, and you can help with that, Raddy. It's all in this carving, because it's got sad eyes."

"Run along," said Grandpa, and they ran along, as if nothing had happened.

16

"STOP RUNNING ME along," said Raddy. "Stop it, Alice. Where are we going?"

"It's not me," said Alice. "I don't know where we're going. Yes I do, it's your shop."

"Not far enough," said Raddy. "We're going to get into the world's biggest trouble. I shouldn't have gone in your church, and that's it. I must have said a prayer out of habit, and that's where the thing went wrong."

"It's going right," said Alice. "Come on. We've got to get back there after the shop."

There was no more time to argue, because running from the Minster to the Market Place took about two minutes, and they were at the shop. The two minutes had not been long enough for Alice to sort out quite what she was doing. She liked to know what she was doing, but everyone does things without knowing why until afterwards. Alice thought that she was doing so much now that there would never be time for her to know why; why she had pulled out a piece of the Minster, which was something she knew she had done because she had seen the hole, and knew that she had not yet done; why she was hurrying Raddy to the shop, something so necessary that it didn't have to be explained, like eating when you feel hungry. But it had to be explained, because they were at the shop.

"Now," said Raddy, "what?"

"Oh," said Alice, realizing what she wanted. "It's that book I want. I want to show it to Grandpa."

"No good running all the way up here," said Raddy, sitting on the ledge at the bottom of the shop window. "I'm all sweat and stitches."

"Well then, walk in and get it," said Alice. "I will."

Maud rapped on the window from inside, and waved Raddy off the ledge. Raddy turned and waved some fingers at her in a sisterly fashion.

"Happen," said Raddy. "It's not here, it's down at home, and I'm not going any further."

"Oh come on," said Alice. "Away." She began to pull at Raddy's sleeve. Raddy pulled back, and her elbow thudded on the glass. Maud came out and told her to give over, the pair of them, it's your fault, speaking first to Raddy and then to Alice. Raddy went back with her into the shop, and Alice followed, determined to make Raddy come with her and deliver the book to her. It was not a question of manners now, but of necessity.

"You can't have it without me," said Raddy, "and I'm not coming; I'm serving in the shop now."

Alice ran out of the shop at once, because she had caught up with herself and knew she was getting angry, and she knew what happened at those times; she knew how many things there were in a shop, and she could imagine for that small amount of time that was needed what a wasteful and ugly confusion would ensue if IT got out of control through her and flung about all the papers and books and cards of pens and bottles of ink and gum and packets of rubber bands and paper clips. It was more than she could bear the responsibility of. She went out, and said "Stop it."

"No," said Raddy, who had come with her to the door.

"You stop it, Alice Dyson. And I'm not going to speak to you again ever, so there. See you on Monday. Goodbye."

"I wasn't telling you to stop it," said Alice. But Raddy had gone into the shop again.

Alice began to run again. She did not know why, and gradually made herself walk instead and felt more sensible without being sure what she was sensible about. But she went on being sensible about it all the way to Raddy's house.

"Where's she trailed off to?" said Mrs Larkman, who was really into the middle of a long scolding of Steve, sitting there in his working clothes and getting in her way. "Get yourself washed, Steve. Up at the shop is she? And give me this week's lodging money, lad. Is she coming back? You don't live here for nowt. I tell you Sissy, that cat isn't a play-toy. You can set and wait if you've a mind to." The last and the first remarks and a bit in the middle had been addressed to Alice, and the rest scattered round the room to others.

Raddy sent me for a book, said Alice's throat, but Alice herself would not allow the lie to come out. "I came for a book," she said. "To borrow."

Mrs Larkman asked her which one, told Steve to hand over his money before he spent it all on beer, told the cat to leave Sissy alone, spoke to the pie she was putting pastry on and said she'd tell our Raddy about borrowing books and not handing them back.

Alice explained more carefully about the book. Steve said she had better go to Raddy's bed and find it but watch out for Barney parading around getting a bath. Mrs Larkman thought, however, that the book (get off the pastry, cat) was one that Raddy (don't you sneak off, Steve) had no right to lend, if it was all the same to Alice (well, I told you, Sissy) and she couldn't have it (leave Bobby alone, he's been an angel all day until you started provoking him) because it was her grandad's and belonged the shop (get Steve to kiss it better).

"He can kiss his own elbow," said Steve.

"But please," said Alice, "I've got to have it quick, for just a minute, because my grandpa wrote it and I want to ask him something and he's just up at the Minster."

Mrs Larkman thought then something that sounded rather complex, involving the cat and Bobby and a pie and Steve, and hearing it was more than Alice could bear, and she was so agitated that Mrs Larkman asked if she wanted the toilet, Alison.

"I suppose I will," said Steve.

"Not dressed like that," said Mrs Larkman, among other things. Alice was not only impatient now, she was frustrated by not knowing what was being said and arranged.

"I'll get our Barney," said Steve.

"The book," said Alice, because she thought she was getting the book, somehow. And in about five minutes' time the book was going with her along the street. She was not allowed to carry it, but she had looked inside and found it was the right edition with the extra stories in. Steve was carrying it, after all, but Barney was with them too, because he was going that way but would not be coming back at once and wouldn't carry the book about all the rest of the day. He thought it might get some beer on it.

"Now then, side up," he said. "We can't carry on at that pace, lass. What's the matter with you? You're that flushed and active, like a germ."

"Please hurry," said Alice. She did not like what was happening. She could feel herself trembling with the effort of carrying on as she was, and the extra work her whole body seemed to be doing was making her hot and sticky and her hair stuck to her face.

"You'll tew yourself," said Barney. "I can't keep with you."

They came up the bank to the Minster. Alice could hardly draw breath now; her ribs seemed unable to bend and stretch as they should, and a hard pain had her in the back between the shoulders.

"You are in a taking," said Steve. "Do you want a jockey?"

Alice thought a piggy-back ride would be undignified, but she had no walk left in her. Steve handed the book to Barney and bent low for her and she rode him the rest of the way to the Minster. His hair smelt of the resiny stuffs plumbers use, and of blowlamps.

Nothing hindered their going into the Minster, but there was no peacefulness within; there was still that same urgent hurry twitching at Alice's heart, tearing at her senses so that nothing she saw or heard was its own self. She could not tell the difference between a sound and its echo, or which came first; she could not tell whether a pillar cast a shadow or whether the shadow grew the pillar.

"I sent you home," said Grandpa, and she saw him afresh, a small grey-haired man sitting at a desk with writing hanging from his pen like smoke.

"I'm still here," said Alice, and wondered what she meant.

"She isn't right well," said Barney. "She was in such a taking we brought her on here."

Alice sat down. There was a chair nearby but she sat on the floor because that was nearer still. Then the room round her moved, but only for her, and she heard herself give something like a groan, the pushing out of breath that accompanies in particular some heavy lifting or holding.

Immediately after it she was well again. The room, the library of the Minster, became what it had been for her at other times, a comfortable house-like place on the shoulder of the Minster with windows looking at the sky and rugs on the floor. She was sitting on one of the rugs.

"I don't know what I did," she said. " IT did."

But the others were not hearing her. They had heard something else and were going to it. She got up and followed them, and wished her foolish clothes were not sticking to her so.

Grandpa and the two Larkman boys had gone to the choirboys' vestry. They stood and looked at what had happened.

One of the cupboards had burst open, both doors standing out. Lifted and yet hunched in the opening were the cassocks and white surplices of the choir, and pushing them out and held by them was the fibre-board backing of the cupboard. From above and below dust had pushed its way out, and behind the fibre-board something still moved a little, the tumbling of small pebbles and grit.

"The place is dropping in bits," said Barney. "You should take more care of your churches, even if you got them for nowt."

"Be careful," said Grandpa. "But I think we'd better have a look."

Steve and Barney lifted away the restraining cloth and let the fibre-board fall to the floor. It whooshed more dust into the vestry, and after it came a shower of decayed mortar and a solitary stone.

"Just the one," said Barney. "It couldn't have come out, for the wall hasn't tumbled below it. It got pushed out."

"There's been noise all morning," said Grandpa. "I thought it was up in the organ loft, but it was in here. Was it the wind?"

"Never," said Barney. "It's gitten shoved, has that."

"Don't touch it," said Grandpa. "Let me look at it." He went to look, squatting down by the stone.

"Don't put your hand in, Grandpa," said Alice. "You know about it."

"I know about it," said Grandpa. "I should never have brought it in. But I thought the Minster would hold it, and it hasn't."

"Wasn't it here always?" said Steve. "I thought most of this had been here always."

"I brought it in," said Grandpa. "I didn't quite understand what it was, and I still don't."

"I understand what it is," said Alice. "Is there a little square opening in it? Where Matthew put his hand."

There was no opening showing, but when Steve and Barney had lifted the stone over it was there.

"Don't touch that part," said Grandpa. "What do you know, Alice?"

"It's Venwath Cross," said Alice. "The one that's lost."

"All but that piece," said Grandpa. "I found that, and I put my hand in that opening, and the terror of that moment has hardly left me since. I put it there, and the wall was plastered over and after fifty years of prayer and torment I had forgotten about it. I am not one of the cathedral clergy, so I did not know the plaster had been taken away, until I heard what happened to Matthew."

"That's my brother," said Alice. "He put his hand in there and got a fright, but he's all right now."

"Did he say what he felt?" said Grandpa. "I dare not ask."

"A hand got hold of him," said Alice. "A hand with a ring on it. I think the stone is in the wrong place, or it would have been worse."

"You go and sit down," said Barney, and he scooped her up, which was just as well because her words had been coming slower and slower and she was falling asleep as she stood. He took her into the library and put her on a chair. But again she preferred the floor and one of the warm rugs, and rolled against a radiator and watched, because sleep was not quite there.

She saw Steve and Barney carry the stone out down the steps, she saw them come back some minutes later, and she heard them banging in the vestry.

Grandpa came in and out with a broom and dustpan, homely things for a Minster: the dustpan was of red plastic.

Then they were all three in the library, and Alice sat up with her back keeping warm. There was an awkward silence, with Steve and Barney wondering how to take their leave, and what had happened to the book they were escorting. They changed their mind about leaving at once when Steve saw the carving on the seat bottom, still lying on the table.

"That's a fancy bit," he said. "I didn't know they had it in those days."

"Oh, aye, it's St Cuthbert Parade," said Barney. "Who's old hookey-nose in the middle?"

"That's a piece of superstitious nonsense," said Grandpa. "I don't know what it is completely, but it's worse than superstitious, because you might have Christian superstition, but that is pagan dressed up to look Christian. I don't know how this girl got to it, because it was fastened up many years ago, when it was found in the crypt below this library and put into its place. It was felt there was something wrong about it, so it was cased in."

"But there's two of them come out," said Barney, "in the one day too? That's not superstition; that's still living."

"It's irreligious and blasphemous," said Grandpa. "Look what they put at the middle of the cross."

"But you don't understand," said Alice. "That isn't Jesus."

"Exactly my complaint," said Grandpa. "Not that I approve highly of any image."

"But it's in your book," said Alice, and she picked the book up and began to open it.

"No," said Grandpa. "It was going to be, but I was so uneasy about it that I left it out and threw away my notes."

"There's a copy," said Alice, and she thought, I know something he does not know; in fact I know a lot he doesn't know. So he hasn't filled the world with everything that can be done.

"Well," said Grandpa, and took the book.

"We'd best be off," said Barney. But Grandpa had the book they were guarding and took no notice of them. He was reading.

"You can't go," said Alice. "Not without your book, and you've got to take that stone to Venwath Cross. Where is it now?"

The stone was in the kirkyard at the moment, with the opening to the ground and two other stones on top of it.

"It's got to get to the proper place," said Alice. "It all makes sense, and it'll be all right if we get it there; there won't be any more trouble."

"We'll not shift off without the book," said Barney. "It's nowt to me or Steve, but our ma said not, and that's it, sithee."

"I *do* see," said Alice. "But there's more and more."

Grandpa had written some more notes down. "You can have the book," he said. "And about this girl, my grand-daughter. I never reckoned much to her until today; she was always a miserable milk-and-water miss, with the milk curdled and the water tepid. But now she's spoken up straight like an honest person, and I'd be pleased if you would do what she wants you to do, because she knows more than I do, and she ought to do what she has in mind."

Alice said to herself that she didn't care what Grandpa thought, but she did, and half, or more, of her caring was from knowing that he was not in fact standing in her way, that she could know and do things he had not already done. Down the steps and through the Minster and out to the kirkyard she held on to Barney's hand and arm, and he had to be a substitute and temporary Grandpa. Then she carried the book, and the two of them carried the stone to the wood-yard, from where, Alice thought, it would be simple to take it in the car to the right place.

"Look after yourself," she said.

"Well, thanks," said Steve.

17

"JUST A PIECE of stone," said Mum. "I looked while Grandpa was with you."

"And you laying on the sofa like Queen Muck giving orders," said Dad. "And not stopped giving them, neither."

"Lying, not laying," said Mum. "She isn't a hen."

"I'm too set in my ways to learn English now," said Dad. "And I'm not a hen; I don't want to be laying that stone anywhere."

"Yes, yes," said Alice. "Please."

"I don't know what set of tales you've got hold of," said Dad. "But if I have to I must. Where is it to go? Up to Sarrow?"

"Venwath," said Alice. "I'll show you on the map."

She and Grandpa had spent some time looking at the map. He had not wanted to look, and had not agreed with anything she had said, but that had not mattered because people don't have to agree to go on talking; in fact they often have to disagree to be able to talk at all. But disagreeing is not the same as being disagreeable, and neither of them had been that.

The map was still on the floor, held flat with books. On it lay two lengths of string. Since no one was holding the ends of the string the pieces formed an irregular cross.

"I don't know what this has got to do with anything,"

said Dad. "I know the bother you've had, because we've had it too. But laiking on with bits of string, what'll that do?"

However, Alice knew what she was doing, though she felt too tired to work it all out and say it. She was more concerned with getting the stone to its proper place.

"This piece of string goes east and west," she said, kneeling on the floor and laying one of them from Lazy Cross to Easter Cross.

"It goes right the length of the Minster," said Dad. "Well, there may be something in that, after all."

"And through the Eyell," said Alice.

"And straight through the Dog and Duck at the corner of the Market Place," said Dad. "Easy with that bit o' band or you'll upscuttle a keg or two."

Alice let the string go and it pulled itself into a wriggle.

"There goes the Angel and the Black Swan," said Dad. "And the Navigator and the Heifer."

"You have to be serious," said Alice. "Please."

"I'm listening," said Dad. "I'm with you, lass."

"Then there's Sarrow Cross," said Alice. "But no one knew where Venwath Cross had got to. Grandpa found a bit lying about and he put it in the Minster because it was funny, it did something to his hand. But, anyway, he thought the Cross was at the bridge, and if you put the other string from Sarrow Cross to the bridge it goes through the Minster, and he sort of thought that was a holy thing to do."

"It clouts the Magdalen pub and the King's Arms," said Dad. "You're spilling a gey lot of ale."

"But I thought it went through the Eyell, and not the Minster," said Alice.

"And that puts it through the Greyhound, and I never did care for that house," said Dad. "Go on."

"Well," said Alice, "simple, Venwath Cross must be on the river Ven."

"Where you cross it," said Dad.

"No, where the Cross was," said Alice. "And that's there."

"It's a bit off the bridge," said Dad, "by a long way. Have you been there?"

"I think so," said Alice. "But I don't know about maps on the ground. Maps show things from higher up than you walk so it isn't easy. But I think I know the place."

"I think I do too," said Dad. "There's a bit of a plantation marked here, but that isn't there any more, and I'll tell you why, because my father cleared all the wood out of that before I was born, and if it had been replanted like he said it should have been I'd have cut it again by now. But I know the spot, and it's a bad one to get at. So you wrap up and get yourselves warm and I'll go round and get the four-wheel-drive with the winch and we'll take it up in that, if I can get it to start."

Alice pulled the strings from the map, pushed the books off it, and it rolled up.

"Grandpa was pleased and not pleased," said Mum. "What was it all about?"

"We decided we didn't like each other," said Alice. "But as soon as we said it we did like each other."

"I told you he loved you," said Mum.

"That's different," said Alice. "Love is me putting nettles on Matthew's knees."

"Is it?" said Mum.

"Well, he doesn't like it," said Alice, "and I get my hands stung but no one gets cross."

"I daresay you're right," said Mum. "But what about you and Grandpa and all this other thing?"

"We'll put the stone back," said Alice. "Grandpa doesn't quite believe about it, but I do. It'll be much better."

"And will that stop the trouble?" said Mum. "I can see a sort of sense in it, if something wanted that stone put back, it might get you to do it. It's not fair, of course, making you do things Grandpa should have done. But is that the end?"

"No," said Alice. "It's more complicated than that, and it'll take ages to do, and Grandpa says it's paganism, you know, believing in things that aren't God, but he thinks there's only one kind of believing, and he wants to say prayers and I won't let him."

"You can't stop prayers," said Mum.

"There's a poor thing," said Alice, "and it came out; I got it out but not on purpose, and I don't like it, and you know what it does. And now it wants to go back and it can't, so I have to help it. But I'm being unkind by not wanting it, but I still want to help it, so that's love, like Grandpa going and getting all those fevers and snake-bites for love of tribesmen that might eat him. So I've shut up the doors against it, and that's horrible for it, but if anyone prays for it that's like throwing stones at it as well and it would be cruel, because it isn't a bad thing. It's like a wolf, that's all, and it isn't right or wrong, so it can't be blamed."

"Well, don't get too soft about it," said Mum. "It's been trouble enough already."

"I'm strong," said Alice.

"Be strong," said Mum. "We'll pray for you. Will that do?"

The four-wheel-drive came to the gate then, with its diesel engine thudding across the twilight. It was the front cab of a towing unit, and usually had the trunks of trees behind it, supported on a separate bogie. Now it was by itself, and Dad was humping the stone on to the small platform at the back.

The cab was cold and cramped and very smelly of old

sandwiches and dogs and cigarettes and beer, on top of the raw diesel and the burnt diesel and the hot oil.

"It's a ramshackle rig," said Dad. Then to smell and vibration was added the howl of the gears, and Alice thought of the wolf she had mentioned a few minutes before. Dad changed gear, waiting to move the stick back until the engine had gone down to a pod-pod-pod rumble and then letting the machine tear its way forward along the road with another kind of yelling from the transmission. Mum covered her ears. Alice drank in the lovely noise.

The journey was short, just to the river Ven, where a sunset lay flat on the water, separated from the sky by land before and beyond.

"Second gate up," they thought Dad said, and that was where he stopped. They had come along a lane, and turned from that. Alice opened the gate for the unit, and it clawed past her in the new mud from the thaw, and there was more sunset in the furrows, notched at the edges by the tyres.

Alice then ran behind the unit, following its red lamps over the track. She knew where she was. This was the way down to the cut in the river bank, where Venwath had been. Dad drove down the nick and stopped with the front wheels in the water, leaving the engine throbbing. Alice came along beside the cut, among brambles and hawthorn and spikes and stings. She looked away from the light, wanting to find the thin ghostly presences she had known before.

They were there. They showed against the sky, or the sky showed through them. They were more distinct than they had been before, and they seemed to see her too.

They want to go back too, thought Alice, and I shall send them back. She pushed into the thicket, but there was nothing to help her, and each step was a struggle.

"You'll get fast," said Dad. "In yon. Is that a cloud of

midges? It can't be this time of year and so cold. What is it? By God, what is it?"

"Oh good," said Alice. "You can see them too. But don't swear, that's only a kind of praying and it might hurt them."

"You mean they're there?" said Dad. "You can see 'em? Well, don't tell your mother I can, or that you can, come to that. We'll pitch that stone out and be off sharp."

"You'll have to go in and put it there with them," said Alice. "That's where the Cross is meant to be."

"Talk sense," said Dad. "With them? But I reckon midges might be worse, and these won't bite. But this isn't where I catch a walking tantrum like yours, is it?"

"No," said Alice, and the thought made her laugh. "We're putting my one to bed."

"If I had one it might be bad for trade," said Dad. "What'll I do, kick a way through?"

Alice said yes, so he kicked a path through, until he kicked a stone, and Alice, just behind, said that was the place.

"Right enough," said Dad, shaking his foot and feeling at the stone with his hand. "It's a bit of mason work, and that'll be the spot. I'll put it here, will that do?"

Alice stood alone by the Cross, surrounded by shadows, partly seen with her eyes, partly made by her eyes; yet Dad could see some of them too. He came back at once with the stone and let it fall in the undergrowth below a hawthorn tree.

"They're still about," he said, looking at the shadows.

"It's only beginning," said Alice.

They went back to the unit, its engine throbbing against the water, and got in. Dad felt in his pocket and took out a couple of coins and spun them into the river. "You've to pay at the wath," he said.

"Superstition," said Mum, but she could hardly be heard,

because the four-wheel drive went in and the unit lifted itself backwards from the water and lurched into the field and stopped.

"Never needed the winch," said Dad, and set the unit forward again.

And now, thought Alice, as the gear noise tore at her, the things are all laid out ready, and all I have to do . . . But she was asleep; and at home had to be carried in. And at all four Crosses communities of shadows waited for her to wake.

18

MUM STOOD IN the Minster library and looked at the carving.

"That's one of the misericords from the choirstalls," she said. "What do you mean, you'll reorganize the St Cuthbert Parade?"

"It's paganism," said Grandpa. "Better forgotten."

"That's the thing, the trouble, IT," said Alice, pointing to the ugly object at the centre of the carving. "That's IT getting fastened away again, and round the edge is the Parade."

"That's no Saint Cuthbert Parade," said Grandpa, "that's a pagan procession, and worse follows bad, you know."

"We don't agree," said Alice. "Do we?"

"No," said Grandpa. "And I agree still less when I look at the manuscripts, because they make it quite clear that the bishops of a thousand years ago were against it too and were trying to have it stopped, and even before that, before St Augustine came to England, because there was Christianity here before that. You must only worship God."

"I'm not worshipping anything," said Alice. "It's just what has to be done, and it works."

"I don't like you meddling with that," said Mum. "But what can I say? ("Nothing," said Alice) I don't care for that figure at all."

"Don't worry about that," said Grandpa. "That's only the carver's imagination. There's nothing like that about."

"I hope it's not like that," said Mum. "But there is something about."

"And I'll deal with it," said Alice. "But don't hurt it, will you?"

"No," said Mum. "And if trying to reorganize the Parade takes your mind off it that'll be a good thing."

"It's just a thing," said Alice, "like money, not good or bad. I'll spend it, that's all."

"It's not very convenient talking about it in the shop, young lady," said Mr Kenroyd, surrounded by his display of lamps and his spools of wire and his dry new kettles and unstarted clocks.

"It used to go a different way," said Alice.

"Not in my time," said Mr Kenroyd. "The circuit is from the Market Place, to Sarrow, down to Easter Cross through Park Street, past the Minster, and back to the Market Place, and that takes long enough and it's hard enough to arrange with the police as it is. And I do what the committee says, not what I decide."

"I'll see the committee," said Alice.

"We don't finish our lessons until six o'clock," said the headmistress of St Hilda's. "Have you come straight from school? As it happens I have ten minutes to spare before I go to a class, so tell me what you have come for."

Alice sat down and told her. "As many people as possible," she said at the end, "and singing hymns and things so that Grandpa doesn't think it is pagan."

"Our girls have never joined in as a school," said the headmistress. "We have never had a float in the procession or anything like that. But what an extraordinary thing to ask, Alice. I thought you had come to tell me about sitting the exam again."

"I might do that, afterwards," said Alice.

"Part of the bargain, is it?" said the headmistress. "Well, what a strange child. All I can do is think about it if I have time. But now I haven't time, because a roomful of girls is waiting for me," and she smiled with her mouth and her neck as well, because that was so wide, and took Alice to the door.

"Enough to do with all the folk coming in afterwards," said Mr Tyle, the Minster verger. "Sweeping up toffee papers and bus tickets, people have no principle respect these days; it was never like it when I began here. Litterate, that's what people are." He was scraping out a candlestick by the high altar.

"It's just about you being on the committee for the Parade," said Alice. "I want it to go a different way round. Grandpa says it used to, and it would be best if it did."

"I daresay," said Mr Tyle. "But you're one bad girl, you know, mischiefing. I'm not a committee, I just do the float for the parish, and that's part the town only, and what's gone on in my time will go on in my time."

"I'll see all the committee," said Alice.

"Waste of *your* time," said Mr Tyle, polishing the candlestick with a damp black smelly rag.

"I'm not in charge of the choir," said Matthew. "I can't make them do anything, and it's no good torturing me because I'm stronger than you now, see."

"You're hurting," said Alice. "You've got your knee on my neck. I won't torture you any more. Tell them they've got to."

"Then they'll torture me," said Matthew.

Alice got up from the floor. Torture had not been a success, but bribery might work. She got down the red piggy bank and shook it. If the money was there she knew how much it was. "Tell them I'll invite them all out to tea afterwards," she said. "That's what boys like."

"Mum will go berserk," said Matthew.

"At a café," said Alice. "I don't pay Mum."

"I'll ask," said Matthew. "Have a fight without torture and I'll beat you."

"I didn't think you'd do anything," said Grandpa. "I wish you wouldn't, in many ways. I'm not on the committee, but my churchwarden, Mr Scaife, is. Don't you go bothering him. I'll tell him what you say."

"You'll put bits of your own in," said Alice.

"No," said Grandpa. "Clergymen learn not to put bits of their own in. You can trust me to say what you want. But Mr Scaife will take no notice of you at all."

"I'm used to that with the committee," said Alice.

"That's committees," said Grandpa. "Alice, how is your visitant?"

"Eh?" said Alice. "Oh, IT. Well, he's quiet but sad, and all he's done lately is tip out Raddy's satchel in the Market Place. He's depressed, you know. He thinks it won't work."

"You get along to the committee, Barney, don't touch that gravy, Freddy, on a Friday, the Father generally sends Mr Larkman but he never goes, Alison," said Mrs Larkman.

"I'll go instead," said Raddy. "Alice could come and we'd count as one."

"Heck ma," said Barney. "A committee. You don't need a committee for a parade; you just go and parade."

"Nowadays you need a committee to tie your shoelaces," said Raddy.

"You do," said her mother, "and another to wash your face, Bobby, let that poker alone, see to him Joe."

"I want Joe as well," said Alice. "I've spent the money in the piggy bank, but I've got some in the real bank."

"Money," said Joe. "I'm on your side."

Alice explained about the choir and the free tea.

"And what do I get?" said Barney.

"Just do as you're told," said Raddy. "I know her. You have to."

"I used to be a Brownie," said Alice. "It wore off. But I couldn't be a scout, and I haven't any money left."

"For this," said the organist, "I speak for the scouts and the guides, so your best way is to become a guide, which isn't very costly, I think." He played a terrible pouncing chord.

"The money is the free tea for obeying, doing what I want," said Alice, when there was a gap in the music he was making.

"Scouts and guides do not take rewards," said the organist. "That's the theory. I could go to the committee, I suppose; but you're not in the same scale as my responsibility; you're a sort of accidental. Are you in any youth movement at all?"

"Childhood," said Alice. His fingers raced up the keyboard.

"Tell me your new route," said the organist. "Then I can show them the score. Why not? Excuse me while I concentrate on this coda," and the notes shot out of the Minster organ in all directions over the heads of the people leaving service.

"I'm not on the committee," said the bishop. "I'm Chance, they're Community Chest; I'm Get out of Jail Free, they're Free Parking. Do you really propose to make them pass Go just when you want? You're not throwing your magic dice now."

"I want them to Advance to Pall Mall," said Alice. "If you said it then they would."

"They wouldn't," said the bishop. "But tell me more."

Alice told him more.

"I'll speak to people unofficially," he said. "They ought not to listen but they do; you know how it is with principalities and powers. And I'll share the cost of the free teas if you are renting all these choirs."

"We'll have it in one of the hotels on Mayfair," said Alice.

"You ride the thing," said Andrea Willis. "I'm not that keen on the job. Well, I used to, you know, but I went off it." Alice wondered what the trick was of making the horse go; she could have driven the four-wheel-drive better.

"I was like that with brownies," she said.

"I was worse," said Andrea. "Brownies don't make you sneeze. I can tell you don't like it much either. Why did you come? He was an hour and a half late coming for you. He'd forgotten, you see. They didn't mean you to come, but I don't mind."

"It's sad for you, not minding me," said Alice. "It's about the parade," and she explained.

"She never said anything at school," said Andrea. "They won't do anything I say, but I'll ride round if you like. Nijinsky will want some tea as well. Sugar lumps will do. Let's put it away and play football where they can't see us."

"Look, you haven't to follow me round to people's houses when I'm working," said Mr Kenroyd, who was feeling under the floor of a bedroom in Mill Lane.

"They think I'm your little girl," said Alice.

"You're not," said Mr Kenroyd. "Just ease the knot out of that cable on the wall, will you? What do you want? If you want me to rewire the Parade it's what I told you before, a job for the committee."

"I've seen most of them," said Alice. "And the bishop. They don't mind."

"Bishops are nothing to me," said Mr Kenroyd. "We don't have them in the Baptists. But I'll go by the committee. Owt else?"

"I want your choir," said Alice. "The other choirs are coming and getting a free tea."

"Our choir isn't children," said Mr Kenroyd, "they'll get their own teas."

"Then that's fixed," said Alice. "Cheaper too."

"They'd rather have the money," said Matthew.

"Did you tell them that?" said Alice.

"I got it out and counted it," said Matthew. "With a knife. I put it all back. They don't think it's enough."

"It's twice as much," said Alice. "The bishop is going shares with me. I should harm you, I think."

"And they said you'd have to write to them about it," said Matthew. "I told you they wouldn't take any notice of me. I don't see why they should take any notice of a girl, either."

"It's the tea," said Alice. "Nothing personal. Dear choir, how do you spell choir?"

"The same as chair," said Matthew. "But different, of course."

"Tuners," said the organist. "They do it better without me, but I can't keep away. Listen."

A note sounded. "Way," called a voice ("In tune," said the organist), and another note was played. "Way," and a third note. "Step back," said the voice ("It wasn't quite so much in tune after all," said the organist). "Way." ("How about your affairs?" said the organist.)

"It's all right about the teas," said Alice. "The bishop is sharing the cost with me."

"It will be rather fun to get a chorus of kids," said the organist. "A full chorus too, if there's enough tea."

"Step back, step back," said the tuner. "Way."

"Get them in too," said the organist, "going backwards. Are you prepared to come to the committee meeting?"

"Um," said Alice. "But I know them all, nearly."

"Get some one to bring you," said the organist. "Now I must go and tell them about those quints; I'm sure they don't break back right."

"I'd better go with *you*, Barney," said Alice.

"He's going with someone already," said Raddy.

"To the committee meeting," said Alice. "If they don't know you're not on it then they won't know I'm not on it."

"Ma put me on," said Barney. "That's official."

"And what hymns have we to sing?" said Joe. "We can't just sing any old hymn. We aren't allowed them all."

"There's nothing like organization, Ruthy have you done that ironing yet I'm waiting to dry the pots, Sissy, take pussy's tail out of Bobby's mouth, you won't manage without a system, Alison," said Mrs Larkman, standing in the middle of her own run-on confusions.

"I haven't enough shelves in my mind, that's all," said Alice. "Half my things are lying on the floor getting trodden on."

"I'm doing more of this than I meant," said Grandpa. "And so are you, aren't you? You need a little notebook. I'll talk to Father Lewis about hymns, and I've talked to Mr Scaife about going a different way, but he hasn't made up his mind. You seem to be in a lot of places these days: I was at the Minster School the other day and you had invited them all to tea, and St Hilda's has a story about you too. And the bishop is worrying about the expense. What expense? He wouldn't say."

"I'm tired of explaining," said Alice. "I don't know whether I've done things or talked about them, and people don't either. They run away when they see me coming."

"And our friend who throws things about, what of him?"

"Moping," said Alice. "He hasn't got a medical brain. He still feels depressed but he isn't getting a chance of doing anything."

"He's going," said Grandpa.

"Not until everything's done properly," said Alice.

Grandpa shook his head. "Heathen," he said.

"You'd best see Miss Bennet," said the policeman, "if it's the same tack again."

"I'll see her anyway," said Alice.

"Let's be having it, then," said the policeman. "The ring."

"There isn't one this time," said Raddy, who had come for company to Alice. The policeman told them to sit down.

Yvonne came through. She stayed her side of the counter. "No one's claimed it yet," she said. "It that it?"

"No," said Alice. "This sounds dafter than that."

"Come through," said Yvonne. "No tricks?"

"Dafter even than that," said Raddy. Miss Bennet smiled.

"It's the Parade," said Alice. "We're having it different this year, and they always get the police about the traffic, so I thought I'd ask you."

"It's right," said Raddy. "She knows how it sounds, but I think she's running it this year."

"I've heard all about you," said Mr Tyle. "They're all on your side, I don't know what you did, but you must be the iron cat inside the velvet kitten. I hear you've got the committee to rights one way and another, and just take your hands off that altar frontal, I can fold it alone, it's my job. I don't know what committees are these days, deciding it all before they've met, no better than the Dean and Chapter, and don't touch that cope, that's precious embroidery done with needles, none of your sewing machine stuff. And it's no good looking at any of the vestments here, you can't have them for your procession, and that's it."

"Mr Tyle," said Alice, "will you be more friendly if I offer you a free tea after the Parade?"

"I'm not unfriendly," said Mr Tyle. "Just outraged."

"Alison Dyerson research ancient documents," said the reporter.

"A, L, I, C, E, next word, D, Y, S, O, N," said Alice. "Just about to strike twelve. This is my friend Miss Bennet."

"Represent?" said the reporter to Alice.

"Me," said Alice. "But I'm quite like my Mum in some ways, and quite like my Dad, if that's what you mean."

"Committee representative various bodies," said the reporter.

"I'm here about traffic," said Yvonne. "That's all."

"Excuse," said the reporter. "More names."

"Come back afterwards," said Yvonne.

"Generally go," said the reporter. "Minutes meeting sent office same each year boring. Meeting operatic society attend same time."

"You stay," said Yvonne. "This isn't the meeting anyone expects."

Mr Scaife was the chairman. He was a large farmer, and his face sloped outwards, cheeks and chin and brow and

nose, and his ears hung over and forward. "Meeting called
to order," he said, and it was like school, everybody became
nearly obedient. Barney came and sat beside her.

"We've lost," he said. "Look at them."

"You've all read the minutes of last year," said Mr Scaife.
"If you haven't read 'em later, but I'll sign now, right?" and
he signed a paper with a large fountain pen. "No comments,
I take it. Finance. We've got quarter of a penny grant from
the council, about a hundred pound. We'll get it spent, never
fear. I think we've got a proposition about some change in
the route, which I'll take now. Where's the proposer?"

Alice was not understanding the course of this at all. She
was not used to meetings of this sort. But she began to understand when she saw faces turn towards her.

"Go on," said Yvonne, "you know them all. You've said
it to them before. Stand up."

Alice stood up. It was impossible to speak, of course, and
no one looked helpful.

"If you've nowt to say, sit down again," said Mr Scaife,
"and make it brief."

Alice thought she would sit down and let the moment go
by. But Yvonne and Barney put their hands against her
back and held her up.

"Don't get twined," said Barney. "Mr Chairman, say."

Mr Chairleg, said her throat, it's spelt like choir only
different. And she thought that if she was not careful there
would be a scene with rr and the Town Hall where they
were would be damaged, and she remembered all the teas
she had promised to pay for.

"Mr Chairman," she said, and all the faces suddenly
smiled at her, and she said what wasn't completely true but
sounded as if it would work well in a meeting, "I have
talked to everyone about this, and they all agree that it
would be better for the procession to be longer this year,

like it was in the old times, and go right round the city boundary, which is where the old Crosses are, and there should be choirs singing as well as people walking about."

"So what do you propose?" said Mr Scaife.

"That," said Alice.

"And who's to organize all that?" said Mr Scaife.

"I've done all that," said Alice.

"Then happen we'd best not vote against it," said Mr Scaife, and Alice was not sure whether she was being laughed at or not. She could not see how Mr Scaife could have been difficult with her, but she saw that Grandpa might have been difficult with him.

"I'll second that proposition," said Mr Tyle.

"Any against?" said Mr Scaife. "Right, that's carried. Sit down lass, you've had your way."

There began a long discussion about the floats, the carts and wagons with displays on them. It was Yvonne that settled the matter by pointing out that the Chief Constable wanted the Parade to start from somewhere else this year because of the nuisance to traffic during a holiday week-end.

"By the Eyell," said Alice to Barney. "That's it."

"Bob up and tell them," said Barney. "Or they'll never stop their clatter and the pubs will be shut."

"I propose," said Alice, because she knew how it was done now, "that the procession begins and ends in Park Street near Eye Street."

"You'll be in the chair next year," said Mr Scaife. "Then we shan't hear so much of you." Alice sat down, thinking she must have spoken too much, but it was more irony, and in fact her proposal seemed sensible to everyone, and it was carried.

The meeting talked on a lot more, and she had to stand up and explain exactly what the route was and where Venwath Cross stood, and go into some detail about the old customs, though she did not know much. However, she had talked to them all so much in the last few weeks that they thought she was an expert.

The meeting ended. The reporter came over. Alice carefully spelt out her name again, and in a wave of generosity said there would be a free tea for all children who went the whole way round all the Crosses and sang at each one. Then she walked home with Yvonne, wondering desperately how you borrowed money from a bank when you had made a foolish promise. But that was nothing much to worry about, because now there was only one thing left, and that was the laying of IT to rest.

19

ALICE WAS NOT alone when she walked through the kirkyard
on the morning of the day of the parade. The yard was full of
shadows of men, women, and children, casting no shadows
themselves, approaching her and looking at her but expecting no response. Some she thought she knew; to see others
was like looking at herself.

It was fate, she thought, or democracy, or some other
mystery, that made this morning, of all those in the year,
that of the St Hilda examination. She was walking there,
as alone as possible, and perhaps it was a good thing to
have a filling for the morning, because by now everything
had been done, and there was only the walk to walk in the
afternoon.

What had been done she could not recall in order. The
arrangements had been difficult beyond her doing alone. A
notebook had not been enough; a computer would have
been better for the detail that had to be ready. Nothing was as
it set out to be; even the great and expensive tea for all
children had grown so large that it had become less and was
now to be a simple matter of orange squash and biscuits in
the Minster hall, with Mr Blackbushe's rubber stamp to put
a purple "PAID" on each left hand as it came in, to prevent
gluttony.

Alice had taken Dad to meetings as her secretary, to help

her get into the right rages at the right times, since other members of the committee, after they had agreed to the changes she had bullied them into, often wanted to slip back into old ways, and she had to keep reminding them of their promises.

"It's what priests do all the time," said the bishop, who had been to two meetings, along with Father Lewis, who was priest at Raddy's church. "Reminding people of their solemn promises. So don't give up, don't look back from the plough."

So Alice had gone on reminding the backsliders of their obligations, until she had them tame enough to know what she meant when she stood up. "Yes," said Mr Kenroyd, once, "you can sit down; I promised: I'll do it," and that got a Baptist choir ready for one of the Crosses, because it was easier for Mr Kenroyd to explain to the choir than try to talk Alice over.

They don't know what I could do if I really looked at them, thought Alice. Or am I making them do it anyway, like throwing dice?

The last meeting was past now. There was nothing more to do but the deed itself. The bishop said that all that was humanly possible had been made ready; now it was the turn of things not human. But there was just the almost human matter of the St Hilda exam. So now Alice walked calmly along on a sunny day, carrying a pencil case and meeting shadows, unable to promise either of them anything.

She was early at St Hilda's. She had to wait in the hall, and saw the other girls as they came in with parents and were left. At first they were only little girls, and then more came of her own age. She thought perhaps she was the only one to have been here before, and felt part of the place already, though not enough to believe in it very strongly.

Outside, the St Hilda girls played tennis. The headmistress

came out of a room and called Alice over to her, taking her away from the rest for a moment.

"This is a busy day for you, I think," she said. "I'm glad you can spare the time. I've been talking to my girls about this afternoon, and some of them think they would like to join in, so they are coming down to Park Street at two o'clock. I shall come down too, because you might need me."

"Shall I?" said Alice.

"I won a town-crier competition," said the headmistress. "I have a very loud voice, and you might need it. Tell me what to shout and I'll shout it."

"I'll think of things for you," said Alice. How manageable, said her throat, turn into a frog. But the frog stayed in her throat and stopped itself from saying itself.

Alice went back to her pencil box and the girls all went into a classroom and sat the exam.

Coming out two hours later she recalled that she had not put her name on the paper at all this time: at first she had not liked to put it in case last year's trick repeated itself, and at last she had forgotten to go back to the top of the first page and fill it in.

Things are decided for me, she thought. That's the democracy bit. So she walked home nameless. She came along Park Street, to avoid the shadows in the kirkyard. No one at all was in the street, but she thought there might have been figures on the Eyell. She went past not looking.

She had been calm during the exam, and calm as she walked home, but once in the house she had nothing to do and began to feel her heart beat to her fingertips, and the coming events began to press on her.

"Easy there," said Dad, when a door or two had banged and she had dropped a plate. "Slow down or you'll split your breeches."

"Can't help it," said Alice. "But it's me doing it, not anyone else; not that thing, you know."

"Seems he might have gone anyroad," said Dad.

"No," said Alice. "Just hoping and moping in a sad way. It's lost, you know," and she felt the presence, mute but alive, and she touched the incomplete ring on her finger; and she wondered what was to happen when she completed the larger ring upon the ground, and whether the two would become one, and whether IT would then stay or go. Because that was not certain: only her own hope was real.

"And how did you frame at Hilda's?" said Dad.

"Middling," said Alice. "I've thought, just this second: if I get the exam I'll go there. I can manage. But if I don't think it's any good when I've been, then I'll change back to where I am now."

"And waste a set of uniform," said Mum. "You wouldn't."

"I'll make them change that," said Alice. "Some of it, anyway," because though she knew her ideas about the uniform were senseless she did not want to make her very own opinion into an orphan.

"You haven't won out yet," said Dad. "So don't pair your socks before they're darned."

"Oh, I don't mind about the socks," said Alice.

"Come to the table," said Mum.

Alice sat at the table, but digestion seemed to have stopped for the day, and she could only look at her plate. "I'll just eat the pattern," she said. But her eye went round and round the rim, where it seemed that all the Crosses lay, and in the middle of the plate a salad Eyell she could not disturb.

At a quarter to two she began to leave the house. "Wait a minute," said Mum. "Toilet."

"Not necessary," said Alice, but she got as far as the gate and had to come back. "It's my last obedience," she said.

"It's the first," said Dad. "We'll come and walk for you when we've washed the pots."

"Good," said Alice. "You can sponsor each other," and she left, taking a cold potato to eat on the way.

People were already gathering to see the floats, but Alice had no eye for them at all. The floats were never going to get to Venwath Cross over the fields. In fact Alice was not sure quite where they would go, because she had only been interested in people on foot. There were no floats or carts on the carving in the choirstalls, and that was the picture she intended to make, people all the way, as the larger circle.

The committee had worked out that parties were to start from the Eyell, though to avoid confusion only Park Street had been named. From there they would go to all four Crosses and spread into the circle from them, leaving the singers at the Crosses to sing. Alice herself had had to leave the organizing because she was going to walk round all the Crosses and finish the ring.

She had an uncanny feeling about a person approaching her. He was dressed in old-fashioned clothes, and she was uneasy because she could not tell whether he was one of the ghosts come very definitely to life and colour, or someone living she knew. It was the bishop.

"I am riding on a cart," he said. "I am Saint Cuthbert. What are you going to do?"

"I am going to walk all the way round," said Alice.

"I shall walk with you later," said the bishop. "In the last part of your walk. Where are you starting and finishing?"

"I don't know where to start from," said Alice. "I've got to do the bit between Easter Cross and Beadlam Cross at Sarrow last of all, so I can start at either of those, and it doesn't matter whether I go up the hill or down the hill first or last."

"You must do it with the sun," said the bishop. "Start at

Easter Cross and go to Venwath, and round that way. I'll
meet you at Beadlam Cross, because I don't think you
should be alone. I'll be your chaplain. But tell me, is this
road Park Lane?"

"Park Street," said Alice.

"Pity," said the bishop. "I could have built a hotel. But
'GO' for you is Easter Cross: most games are played the lucky
way round."

Alice's town crier found her next, trailed by some of the
girls of St Hilda's. "Shall I shout?" said the headmistress.
"Where should the girls go?"

Alice handed them over to Barney, who had Steve and the
rest of the Larkman family with him to keep order. "I never
saw so many folk," he said. "Aye, we could do with a
shouter; come this way, Missus," and the girls giggled and
then laughed. Alice had expected that they would only
giggle.

Then there was something going a little wrong with the
crowd of people assembling. There was quite plainly some
sort of sad happiness beginning, and people were turning to
others and exclaiming and looking startled.

"Hey up," said Barney. "What's amiss?" and he felt the
people he was trying to arrange were taking their attention
away and looking at the past remembering itself before their
eyes. "Now, reverend mister," he said to the bishop,
"they're getting away of me." He found his own priest near
at hand as well. "Father," he said, "bring them back."

"Something is stirring," said the bishop. "I will talk to
them. Help me up on a cart, and bring Father Lewis too."

Between them, he and Father Lewis began to gather the
crowd together again. At first they had little success, but
Alice went to the headmistress of St Hilda's and said, "Go
and help Barney. I mean, please go and help Barney. Shout
for order."

"They're not all people," said the headmistress. "You girls stay with me; there's nothing to worry about. Alice Dyson isn't worrying."

"It's mostly ghosts," said Alice. "Sort of. Don't talk to them, they're probably Anglo-Saxon." She stood herself aside and saw the people begin to listen and become calmer.

Now there was nothing she could do here; she was just one of the kids among the rest and could do nothing useful. She thought she had better start her journey, and slipped away up the road and along towards Easter Cross.

She did not go alone. She was followed from the crowd, first by Raddy, who had been looking for her, and then by other figures less distinct. She had been looked at before, and approached, but this was the first time she had been followed. Now she was sure that something was beginning to work.

"Wait on," said Raddy. "You go such a gallop, and it's got so hot and close, it's demming in for something like thunder after a grand morning: it isn't sunny any more."

Clouds were gathering overhead, but further away, out of town, sunshine still was the crop standing in the fields. On Alice her sweat began to stand like dew.

"I have to hurry," she said. "And I've got a potato stuck on the edge of my stomach and it won't swallow down."

"Let the others catch up," said Raddy. "It's a stitch you've got." But when she looked round she saw no one. "There was a lady down there saw her sister that died last year, and she was all fainty about it."

"She should look where she's going," said Alice. "And she's not the only one. What's the cure for potato-clag?"

"Peel it first," said Raddy. "Here's Easter Cross. Which way?"

Alice felt like turning to Sarrow Hill and Beadlam Cross; she was pulled that way, towards completeness, and the part ring on her hand throbbed. But that would finish the circle too soon: the people had to be there when she came back to Easter Cross; that larger circle had to be ready first, the circle that would bind the thing down, not the one that would bind her.

She and Raddy turned towards Venwath and hurried, because the circle had to be complete, still there, still full, when she was back at Easter Cross again. It was not going to be a walk, even a fast one, she realized; it was going to be a run, and one she had not been able to rehearse. The potato was agony.

Steve had come the day before, with Dad, and cleared a way down by the river so that it was possible to walk to the place of the Cross and go past. They went past all the people living, but met those long dead too. At the Cross they saw sunshine beyond the river, but Alice had to turn from those calm prospects back into the darkness gathering over the town under the cloud. She could see from this place outside the houses that the darkness stood only on the city, and that there was repose all round.

"I keep seeing people," said Raddy.

"Clouds of midges," said Alice, hoping to keep her companion with her longer.

"With faces?" said Raddy. "Go on, now where?"

"Lazy Cross," said Alice. "That'll be half way. When the people get all round they're supposed to stop quarter of an hour: they have to. And the people at the Crosses sing."

"Yes," said Raddy. "Our lot was at Venwath, but you took no gaum."

"Never saw," said Alice. "Away, Raddy."

Lazy Cross was by the bishop's house, in the town. The bishop's house had once been the leprosy hospital. Alice and Raddy came out of the fields and sweated along streets, passing gathering crowds that did not know the necessary journey of the hurrying girl.

"Some of them aren't real," said Raddy. "They aren't. But I'll know one of them soon, I'm sure, and then what?"

"Don't worry," said Alice. "We'll get round in time and that's all we need. Then they'll go back."

"Promise?" said Raddy. "It's them or me, isn't it? Father Lewis said it was all right back there, but the lady fainted, didn't she? and I might faint too. But I'll go down on my backside and not get hurt."

"It'll be right," said Alice. "Shut up."

At Lazy Cross there was the Minster choir with the organist, singing psalms, very like a street concert. No one had thought that twilight would come in the middle of the day, and the boys had to read the words by the light of house windows behind them. Matthew stepped from his place at the end of the line, and with his shiniest beamingest face sang a word at Alice and bumped her on the back and went to his place again. Alice thought he must have been told to do it, since none of the choir looked at him and he seemed so ready. She was pleased, but had no breath to let even her throat respond.

The sound dropped away as she went on up the hill towards Sarrow and Beadlam Cross. On the way they met the floats. Alice paused a moment and saw that too many people were with them, and she was sure they should be in the great circle. But there was nothing she could do but hurry on again. As she went, hotter and hotter, her hand aching under the tightening grip of the ring, she saw the way lined with waiting figures, and understood that they were the ghosts, for the most part, assembling in the circle and part of it, waiting to go home again at the end.

"Goodbye," said Raddy, before the top of the hill. She stopped walking. "I'm off home."

"Stand there," said Alice. "Stand."

"I'll lay down," said Raddy, and sat on the kerb against a street lamp in the dusk. At that moment the darkness was deep enough for the lamp to come on as if it were true night. "I's frightened," said Raddy.

"Pray," said Alice. "Not for me, though."

"I'm beyond that," said Raddy. "I'll go as I am."

Alice hurried on. At Beadlam Cross there stood Grandpa, bearing his part in the circle, and with him Mr Scaife, shadows in twilight among other shadows.

Alice smiled at Grandpa, but she thought her face did not move. She touched the Cross with her right hand, and saw upon her finger a dark gold ring, apparent but still unfinished. She saw and felt and turned it. The light that showed it to her came from outside the town where it was still full day. She paused a moment and took in a hot breath and thought she breathed out a cooler one. Her legs shook as she stood and all her muscles twitched. Her eyes began to rattle in her head, she thought, but with them she could still see, and saw again the Minster standing roofless against the grey sky, and once more the Eyell stark against the fields, but crowned now with a thread of darkness coiling to the blackness overhead. All over the city house lights were on, and a bus turned a corner glaring headlamps and glowing tail lights, illuminated within.

A shadow came near, large on the day side of her. Andrea Willis was there nervously on a nervous pony. "He won't go nearer," she said. "Neither of us."

On the other side a smaller figure approached. It was the bishop, and following him Father Lewis. Alice did not speak, but moved on; movement stopped the random pull of her muscles. Here was her chaplain for the last sector of the circle, and she went on with him, or with two of them, and left the choir, probably Mr Kenroyd's Baptists, to grow fainter at Beadlam. Now she was hurrying downhill, and as she went she felt the ring complete itself, and looked down and saw it doing so, and she was glad she had her chaplain with her because here might be starting something more than she could deal with.

Then there was singing ahead, and the way was lined with people from all times, and she knew the greater circle had been complete upon the ground before the ring had been complete on her finger; but for all that she was unsure of what was to come.

It was clear at Easter Cross, in the darkness that she still had choices, as she had had all winter and spring. She stood making the choices in a wide-spaced rain that had begun to fall on her.

She had made the great circle, and the smaller one had been made on her. She could now keep the ring and with it keep everything, including IT; but IT was what she had to be rid of. But now, at last, she was true master of IT.

So she hesitated, whether to keep power or keep right. Though IT was not right or wrong, she could herself do right or wrong. And she now knew that IT did not mind whether it slept again, or woke into strength with her.

Complete darkness came like midnight upon her. The rain closed up, and to stand in it was like being in a waterfall. All round her shadows solidified so that she could not tell the grainy ghosts she had experienced from the plain people she knew. But on either side, and touching her, stood Father Lewis and the bishop, and through them she could still tell, even in the dark, what was real; and she knew what was to be done.

She held out her hand, and from the ring there flashed the reflection of a ribbon of lightning that struck from side to side of the cloud. The ring was now the centre of all, and the weight of the world seemed to be on it. She put her other hand to it and turned it on the finger, and then drew away the hand that wore it. It was now ringless, free. In the ring was all the pull of darkness for ever encircled by it: to look at it was like looking into the opening on the stone in the Eyell, substance and not substance, place and not place, time and not time. The darkness looked back as if it were an eye: eye or Eyell. She carried it, and it was like carrying a gyroscope with its unwillingness to conform to gravity, and took it to the opening on Easter Cross, which was the same as coming to the opening at the Eyell, and pushed it against the corresponding darkness that had come there, darkness unlike the absence of light on the afternoon midnight.

The ring and the opening became one, and then became nothing, and there was only stone. The ring itself fell for ever away from her hand, down into the bottom of time, dwindling without diminishing, along a perspective of eternity.

Thunder began in the cloud, rolling from edge to edge, and the rain washed down and stood underfoot and flowed in the gutters. Through it people stamped, splashing, and among them ghosts moved, without splashing, all in one direction, towards the Eyell, men, women, children, another flow entirely. In with the thunder came the calling of the Minster bells. The high of their tune, and the low of the thunder rang separate and together.

The edges of the cloud over the town shrank in. At Easter Cross there was sunshine, and Alice and her two chaplains grew a joined three part shadow. Alice found herself shaking in daylight, but no longer twitching. Beside her the bishop took off a wet medieval garment and smiled. But Alice was looking towards the middle of the town, where the Minster still stood in the dark. Above it the cloud still hung, covering it and the Eyell. Some of the darkness was not cloud at all, but the being of IT become visible, complete in IT's shape like the carving from the Minster. Then that part of the cloud shrank away and sank and ran down small into the Eyell, taking the heaviness of the dark with it and leaving only cloud.

"It has simply gone. Oh, that potato," said Alice, and she was suddenly and copiously sick in the running gutter where she stood, and her hot sweat turned cold on her back, weight went from her, and another kind of darkness again rose behind her eyes, so that the bishop and Father Lewis had to hold her. She was brought a great cup of water from a house, and before she put it to her mouth Father Lewis held it and the bishop blessed it, making it holy water. She rinsed her mouth with it, and swallowed a little, and with the rest her two chaplains soaked a cloth and washed her face and her hands, talking quietly to themselves, one in English, the other in Latin, but saying the same thing.

"We are praying for you now," said the bishop. "You have lost one possession and no others must take its place."

"I am now perfectly well," said Alice. "Thank you very much. I'm going to have my tea, that we promised the kids."

They walked on into the town, where it still rained but now the thunder had stopped. Alice had her hand stamped "PAID" like other children and had her biscuits and orange squash, alone in herself. Children ran outside after their teas and washed the ink off in the rain.

"He should stamp their backsides," said Raddy. "They wouldn't hang that out to get washed off."

Mum and Dad found Alice at last, taking over from the bishop and Father Lewis. "And is it all right?" said Mum. "You look a bit pale. Grandpa's just coming along too."

"Grand," said Alice, giving her a kiss, holding Grandpa's hand, and leaning on Dad.

"Now," said Dad, because he wasn't able to be quiet.

"We had that strapping lass from Hilda's round saying they'd take you next back end."

"Autumn," said Mum.

"Happen," said Dad. "But no more common talk like 'grand'. Say 'excellent' or summat."

"I'll think on," said Alice. "I've sweated cobwebs enough for today."